An Anthology of Short Stories

ALSO BY PAUL B KOHLER

Linear Shift, Part 1
Linear Shift, Part 2

Borrowed Souls

Silo Saga: Recoil

Something to Read on the Ride:
    A Charity Anthology
    Amy (contributed)

Something for the Journey:
    A Charity Anthology
    Gold Rush (contributed)
    Lookout Mountain (contributed)

Something to Take on the Trip:
    A Charity Anthology
    Alone (contributed)

AN ANTHOLOGY OF SHORT STORIES

PAUL B. KOHLER

SUMMER 2014

Edited by David Gatewood, Kyle Hooper,
Amy Maddox, and Carol Davis

Cover design by Paul B. Kohler
Interior design and layout by Paul B. Kohler

ISBN-13: 978-1-940740-03-4
ISBN-10: 1-940740-03-7

www.paul-kohler.net

Give feedback on the book at:
info@paul-kohler.net
Twitter: @PaulBKohler
Facebook: facebook.com/Paul.B.Kohler.Author

Printed in the United States of America

First Edition

For all fans of short fiction

Table of Contents

AMY

A TRAGIC ADVENTURE

PAUL B. KOHLER

A toddler's independent adventure leads to a tragic and unexpected end.

Amy was my first trip into fiction writing, and it sat untouched for nearly 15 years before I dusted it off, gave it a quick polish and submitted it to be included in Something to Read on the Ride : A Charity Anthology. It was accepted in September of 2013, and is still in print.

AMY

Amy was just two years old, and needed to be a part of everything. All she wanted to do was explore her surroundings. *How does this work? What's over there? Or, what's that over there, by that thing?*

Her parents left her inside while they went out to shovel snow. Tending to the weather was hard enough; adding a toddler to deal with would have been just too much. Amy didn't mind though. It gave her time to investigate the places where she wasn't supposed to be. Her favorite place was the place where she took her bath. It was fun. That special place had a big mirror on the back of the door. She liked to go in and close the door behind her. She spent hours in front of that mirror. Everything she did, the girl in the mirror did identically. *Was it magic? Who was behind the door? Why did she look like me?* All the questions went unanswered.

That's not why Amy went into the bathroom today. She wanted to know what was behind the small doors beneath the sink. The doors would never open. No matter how hard she pulled, they would never open more than a crack. Her mom and dad could open them all the way, but they always closed them before Amy could see what was inside.

The doors in the kitchen, that were just like them, always opened easily. Plus, there was always stuff to play with inside. Pots, Pans, books, and boxes. She loved to pull everything out of the cabinets and climb in to play hide and seek with her daddy. It was one of her favorite things to do.

How did they do it? she wondered. She ran to the doors and with her tiny hands on the knobs, pulled both doors at the same time. Nothing. She pulled harder, grunting. She thought she had felt them budge, but her little hands slipped off the handles, and she went tumbling backwards. The doors refused to share their innocent secret. Amy got back up, pouting, and moved back over to the cabinet. She gripped one handle and gently pulled open the door as far as it would go, trying to peek inside. It was really dark in there.

Wait, what was that at the top of the door? It looked like something or someone was holding the door shut from the inside. She tried to touch the mysterious white latch, but the door pinched her fingers when she leaned against it. "WOAA" she cried. Whatever was behind the doors, bites.

Amy became bored with the tiresome doors and went to play with the big water chair. She watched her mom and dad use it all the time. They would first lift up the cover, then sit down. Well, mommy always sat down. Daddy sometimes stood. After sitting for a while they would stand up, get dressed again, and push the little silver button. *WHOOSH!!* She thought that was so neat, and decided to try it herself.

First, she tried to lift up the lid. The weight of the lid surprised her, and it took both of her hands to get it all the way up. Up. Up.

There!

Once the lid was open, Amy began playing with the water inside the bowl. *If I only had my little rubber ducky...* She mused.

5

Amy's hands were getting cold from the water, so she reached up and pushed the silver button.

WHOOSH!! All the water went away down the drain. *Wait, it's filling up again. How does that work?* She reached up again and pushed the silver button. WHOOSH!! This time she giggled. WHOOSH!! WHOOSH!! She giggled uncontrollably. *This thing makes the funniest noises.*

Then she focused on the defiant doors again. *How could she get those doors open?* She pulled one of the doors open from the top this time, and when her little wet hand slipped behind the door, it must have knocked whatever was holding the door shut, loose. The door was now open all the way.

Amy sat down in front of the cabinet, anxious to see inside. The cabinet was filled with all sorts of wondrous things. Things she had never seen before. She grabbed the first thing that caught her eye. It was a big stick attached to an upside down rubber bowl. She turned it over and, as with everything else that she grabbed, put it in her mouth.

YUCK... That's not very good. Realizing that it smelled just as bad as it tasted, she quickly dropped it on the floor next to her.

With that out of the way, she noticed

several rolls of soft white tissue paper. She knew what these were. Her mom and dad always yelled at her whenever she pulled down on the roll that hung next to the water chair. Amy didn't like getting yelled at so she just pushed them aside.

What was that behind the rolls? Towards the back was a bottle with a picture on it. It was a picture of a bald, muscular man with his arms crossed, wearing an earring and a white T-shirt.

Was he smiling at me? She wondered, but she couldn't tell because the bottle was too far away. She thought if she could only reach the bottle, all her questions would be answered. She stretched out as far as she could, but her infant arm was not long enough to reach it.

Amy realized she could fit inside the cabinet, like the ones in the kitchen. She stood up, turned around, took a few steps backwards, and then plopped down, right into the cabinet.

Yippee, I'm in!

Once inside, she looked at the back of the door and saw what had been holding it shut. It was a thin piece of plastic at the top edge. She reached up to grab it so she could break it off. As she yanked it to her, the door followed.

"WOAA", she screamed as the door pinched her little fingers, again.

She would have normally been scared by her new found darkness, if she hadn't gotten used to playing hide and seek with daddy. She thought she was so sly, and she began to snicker. Amy sat there in the dark for a long minute waiting for her daddy to come find her. *Where is he?* She wondered.

"Daddy", she called out for him.

No response. She called out again, but louder this time. "DADDY". Still nothing.

She decided to go find him instead, and tried to push the door open. The door only opened a crack, then closed again. She tried the other door, but got the same result. Frustrated, she tried both doors at the same time. Again, she had no success.

She was beginning to get scared of the darkness and started to whimper. She tried to stand up and immediately struck her head on the bottom of the sink. She started to cry and called for her parents.

"Mommy!" sniffle "Daddy!"

The tears started rolling down her pinkish cheeks, and dropping into her lap. She wondered why they weren't coming. Her parents usually ran to her and gave her lots of love and attention whenever she started to cry. Amy knew this, and she began to cry louder and louder.

Amy began to worry, *Why won't they come?*

She couldn't remember doing anything bad, or anything that she should be punished for. A moment later, Amy thought she heard something. She again tried to stand up, and struck her precious head on the bottom of the sink. This time it hurt worse than the first time. She reached up to soothe her aching head. When her hand got to the growing bump, she felt wetness in her hair.

It was too dark in the cabinet to notice that the moisture on her head was not water, but her own blood oozing from a cut. An exposed screw, used to attach the sink to the cabinet, sliced her head.

Amy started to panic and began to pound her little hands on anything she could reach. Each strike of her hands, caused a loud 'Thud' or 'Smack'. Along with her hysterical crying and screams, the noises were starting to hurt her eardrums. She continued to throw her arms around frantically, trying to break free from this cage she was in, knocking over bottles and jars.

After what seemed like an eternity, she

stopped pounding her fists on the doors, due to exhaustion. Her once squeaky voice was now hoarse from the screaming and crying. The knuckles on her fingers had swelled up and were coated with blood. *How long have I been in here?* she wondered. It seemed like forever to her.

Amy's once soft, long blonde hair was now soaked with blood that had drained from the cut on her head. The coagulated blood had formed into a large gob of dark red goo.

Her crying weakened to a muffled sob; she began to get dizzy. *What was going on?* she thought. She started to lose control of her balance and her eyelids were feeling very heavy. She fought to maintain consciousness, but her clouded mind was losing its' grip of reality. She visualized her parents in her mind for the last time. She missed them so.

Amy tried one last time to call out for them. "Mooommy", "Daady". Her quiet little voice went unheard as she lost her battle to stay awake, and slipped into silence.

PAUL B KOHLER

RUINED
SACRIFICE

A SHORT STORY

Newlyweds James and Alison are on the trip of a lifetime, trekking through the jungle exploring ancient pyramids. Told that a number of interesting structures are off limits, they decide to wander off on their own ... only to discover that they're not alone — and that the ancient past has a dangerous habit of springing back to life!

Ruined Sacrifice is my latest short story, and this is the first publication including it. I started writing this story after touring a Mayan ruin site in June 2014. Hearing about the ancient life and climbing an actual pyramid were very inspiring to the story line.

RUINED SACRIFICE

The day was sweltering, the air near body temperature and still. The morning had overcast skies that threatened cooling rains, but now the humidity was near saturation. Ever_ the guide looked stifled. The jungle seemed to weep the hot wetness of life itself.

It was just before noon when James and Alison arrived at the base of the pyramid. Their tour guide had spent the better part of two hours leading them through the front half of the archaeological site, stopping briefly along the way to enlighten them on the historical significance of the ancient race. At each stop, both James's and Alison's eyes were drawn to the towering structure located at the center of the ruined city.

From a distance, it appeared to rise just above the jungle canopy, but only by a small, indistinguishable amount. As they stood at its base, staring up the steep incline of the jagged steps, it looked much taller than either of them could comprehend.

"And here. The Islaxa Temple Pyramid," Arturo, their day guide, said as he motioned to the mountainous structure. "It was discovered in 1976, and after 12 years of digging, it opened to the public."

"Why'd the dig take so long?" asked Alison.

"Things move slower down here than what you're probably used to in the United States. Funding is the biggest obstacle. Once financial backing was in place, the university had to find an appropriate number of skilled workers to carry out the dig. As of today, only about forty percent of the site has been rediscovered," Arturo said.

James whistled. "Only forty?"

"Yes. You've certainly noticed the ropes suspended along the boundary? They're not just there for your safety. They represent the extent of archaeological discovery on the site. New funding is being collected right now for the next phase," Arturo replied.

"What exactly is the next phase?" asked

Alison.

"There've been thirteen structures discovered up to this point, and you've passed by most of them already today. There are an estimated fifteen to twenty additional structures waiting to be unearthed to the south."

His interest piqued, James asked, "Can we see those ruins ... in their undisturbed state?"

"No, I'm afraid not. The terrain to the south has yet to be declared safe for visitors. There are dangers in the jungle. Dangers you may not fully comprehend," Arturo said.

"Come now. Are you afraid we'll trip and fall over some tree root and twist an ankle?" asked James.

"Partly, señor. With no trails in place, you may in fact encounter walking hazards. But it's mostly the unseen dangers that would likely harm you," Arturo said. "Now, if you would like to climb the pyramid, please ..."

"Hold on a sec. Unseen dangers? Would you care to clarify?" asked Alison, equally intrigued by the adventurous nature of this part of the world.

"Well – I'm not really supposed to encourage interest in that part of the property, señora, but I can expand on a few points if you wish."

"We wish," James and Alison said in unison.

Arturo hesitated briefly before continuing. "When this site was first discovered in the Seventies, several explorers were lost to what we call *trampa*. It means *deadfall* in your language."

James nodded his head in understanding, as part of his thesis had dealt significantly with archaic trapping pits.

"In the base of each trampa were sharpened stakes protruding up. Many of the early scouts explored solo, and once they fell into the pit, they were impaled and had no way of calling for help. Most of the pits have been filled in, but we cannot guarantee that they were all discovered." Arturo cleared his throat before continuing. "Then there is the threat of wildlife. The jungle is teeming with ..."

"Spider monkeys. You mentioned that earlier," Alison said.

"Oh, no, señora. True, there are monkeys in the jungle, but they are relatively harmless. It's the Cantil snake that's the problem."

"Wait, isn't the Cantil indigenous to the northern part of the peninsula?" James asked.

"This is also true, but there have been more than a hundred sightings in and around the ruins in the past year alone. They are very poisonous, señor."

"Just how poisonous?" Alison asked.

"You probably won't die from a bite, but a tour guide nearly lost his leg three months ago when he was bitten just inside the restricted area." Arturo's face showed concern. "Please, señor and señora. Do not explore beyond the rope. It is for your own safety."

"I think we'll stick to the marked trails from here on out, Arturo." James patted the guide on the shoulder, then reached into his pocket and pulled out a handful of pesos. "Here. Take this as our thanks for all your information. We're going to climb the pyramid and then take our time heading back through the ruins we passed on the way in."

"Gracias, señor. If you need anything else, I will be near the entry where we picked up the maps."

With that, Arturo left them to climb the forty-meter-high temple.

***

James and Alison climbed the ancient ruin, not hand in hand, but cautiously, with both hands on the steps in front of them so as to not fall backward because of the considerable steepness of the historic monument.

Each step was different from the last in every aspect of the climb. The height and depth of each tread had deteriorated over thousands of years by both the erosion of human traffic and being assaulted by nature's harsh elements of wind and humidity. The pyramid they were climbing was one of only a few left in the world that were still open to the public, and only one face of the pyramid was accessible.

James thought about the last time those primordial steps had been ascended. Some form of ritual ceremony came to mind. Maybe it was to make some kind of dole to a king? Or could it have been by a couple like him and Alison who had recently vowed their love for one another, and engaged in wholly matrimony? *Did kings perform those kinds of ceremonies back then?* he wondered.

As they neared the halfway point of the steep climb, James stood straight up and turned to look down to the base of the structure. His knees weakened briefly at the sight but he quickly regained his balance. The view was awe-inspiring. Alison followed a few steps behind and came to rest next to James.

"Would you look at that," Alison said as her eyes swept across the treetops of the jungle surrounding the pyramid.

"It takes your breath away," he said as he slid his fingers into hers. "I love you, baby."

She squeezed his hand in return and looked into his eyes. "Thank you for such a wonderful trip. This is the most perfect honeymoon I could have ever imagined."

"Only the best for my wife," he said, feeling proud to finally say the word.

Now, here they were – on the trip of their dreams, to visit a ruined city in the Mayan jungle. Having both graduated with a degree in archeology, but neither practicing in the field, their visiting a site that had been only discovered 40 years previously was, in fact, the trip of a lifetime.

With a final squeeze of Alison's hand, James said, "Let's finish the climb, babe. It's not getting any cooler out here."

"I think it's actually getting hotter," Alison said as she wiped a bead of sweat from her forehead.

James returned to the four-point

climbing stance that had been working for him so well. As he continued his ascent, he couldn't help but look out across the treetops every few steps. Distracted by the vast beauty of the lush forest beyond, he misjudged a step and dragged his toe across the edge of the stone face. The rhythmic nature of his climb made him lift his other foot before his first foot was firmly placed on the step above, causing him to falter and drop to his knees.

"Easy, honey. It's not a race to the top," chided Alison.

"Yeah, I know. The view is just so phenomenal, and I lost track."

Throughout the rest of the climb, both he and Alison focused on the uneven nature of the steps. Within fifteen minutes, they reached the first plateau of the pyramid. The tier was some eight steps below the top visiting platform – which was practically full of other site visitors. James wasn't a fan of crowds, so he lowered himself onto his haunches and waited for some of the sightseers to begin their descent. Alison had no such reservations to strangers and climbed the remaining steps to the top.

The wait wasn't bad for James, though, as it gave him a chance to take in the beauty of the enormous jungle. In the distance, he noted a few of the other structures peeking out above the canopy and wondered if the tree growth was consistent throughout the region. He tried to imagine what the city would have been like in its day. As he sat in contemplation, the time passed without notice.

Suddenly, out of the corner of his eye, James noticed an elderly woman nearly slip off the top step. He sprang to his feet and caught her arm before she lost her balance and began a certainly fatal tumble down the face of the pyramid.

"Easy, there. The beauty's really something, but it's not worth harming yourself over," James said as he led her away from the platform edge.

"Oh, my. I don't know what happened there. It felt as if I was being pulled to the edge without any control," she said. "If it weren't for your quickness ... well, I'm not sure where I'd be right now. Thank you."

"Don't mention it. Do you need help getting down? The steps can be pretty treacherous."

"How gracious of you to ask, but no, I'll be fine," she said before turning and taking her first step off the edge with ease.

When James turned to look at the upper

platform he found Alison sitting on the highest edge with her legs dangling over. He smiled at her and climbed up to meet her.

"So, are you Superman all the time, or just to frail old ladies in need?" Alison asked.

"Hey. She could have really hurt herself there. Come to think of it, I'm quite surprised that they have this open to the public. There are no safety rails to speak of up here," James said as he sat next to her.

"Well, we'd better alert the management right away!" Alison said.

"Joke now, but mark my words – the Mexican government will be sued within the year by the family of a falling victim on those stairs."

Alison slid her arm into James's and leaned her head against his shoulder. "It really is something," she said, looking toward the jungle.

"That it is. At least we have a breeze up here. I can't imagine the king, or whatever he was, living up here."

"No, dear. I think you misunderstood. I think Arturo said he only stayed up here when he was called upon by other city leaders."

"That makes more sense, Mitz, but I could have sworn that he told us the king stayed up here for long periods of time. See?" James motioned to the roped-off room behind them. "That's where he slept when he was up here "

Alison glanced back to the small stone chamber. "Hmm. Maybe. I don't think it's that important that we miss a few of the details on our trip." She turned back to the jungle below and asked, "Are those the structures we passed on the way to the pyramid?"

"Yeah, I think that one was the shrine," James said, pointing to his left. "And that one was the residence hall." He swung his finger to the right. The two structures looked like grey lumps in an otherwise flat carpet of greenery.

"Hey! While you were taking your nap, I looked around up here. I've got to show you something," Alison said.

"Napping? Really?" James gaped sarcastically.

Alison swung her feet around and stood, pulling James along.

They first stopped next to the chamber at the center of the platform. The room was quite small.

"How could someone live in there?" asked James. "It's no bigger than an elevator car."

"Maybe it *was* an elevator, and it goes down to a full apartment deep inside the pyramid," Alison joked. "Seriously, though, you've got to see this."

She pulled on his arm and led him around the back side of the king's chamber. As they made their way, another boundary rope stopped their progress. Without hesitation, Alison lifted her leg over the rope and continued to pull James with her.

"Hey, babe. I don't think we're supposed to be back here," James protested, but only mildly. He was just as intrigued to see everything they could as she was.

"It's alright. I was back here earlier, and there's something you need to ..."

Alison's voice trailed off as James looked out over the southern exposure of the jungle. From their height, he could see several raised mounds of greenery in the distance.

"Those must be the unexcavated structures Arturo was talking about," James said.

"Yeah, and it looks to be larger than this one," Alison said, pointing to one that was directly south.

"How far do you think?" James asked.

"Hmm. From the base of this pyramid, I'd guess no more than two, maybe three miles,"

Alison said. "Are you thinking what I'm thinking?"

"You know, great minds think alike, and all that." James winked at his bride. "Do you think we can duck out unseen?"

"I've got an idea that might work in our favor. Let's get down from here and follow my cue," Alison said before kissing James on the cheek and returning over the boundary rope.

***

Twenty minutes later, James stepped off the final tread of the pyramid, following Alison's lead. The pyramid faced due north, and there were the familiar boundary ropes leading to the east and west, gently curving back toward the site entry. It was clear that they were as far south as the site had been excavated. James looked around the clearing directly in front of the pyramid and his hopes of sneaking away vanished. In his estimation, there were nearly fifty other temple visitors nearby, along with their accompanying guides. If it had been just the other visitors, he and Alison could easily get away from the crowd unnoticed. It was the guides that worried him.

Alison, on the other hand, was unphased

by the crowd as she began making her way back to the western trail they'd taken to come here. James followed her through the approaching crowd. As they left the clearing, the crowd thinned. Alison slowed her pace as the trail turned to the north. James saw only a handful of visitors moving their way before the trail curved out of sight.

"Once this group passes, we should be able to hop over and duck into the jungle and out of sight before the next group comes around the bend," Alison said.

James nodded. "Yeah, I think you're right. Nice job, babe."

"I have my moments," Alison said as she leaned into James for a long embrace as the approaching group moved by them. As the group passed, Alison released James and began to walk north up the trail a few more yards.

James followed, glancing in both directions. "It's clear," he said as he stepped over the rope, holding out his hand to help Alison over.

"Thank you, dear," Alison said as she took his hand and hopped over the rope.

Once over, they made a quick jaunt in the best direction away from the trail. Only when they were concealed by the jungle growth did they turn to the south and begin their hike towards their destination. James led, with Alison following some ten paces behind, so as not to get hit in the face by tree branches moved by James.

After a while of hiking in silence, Alison called out, "Are we on the right course?"

James pulled his pack off, unzipped the side pocket and fished around until he found his travel compass. By the time he had it out and level, Alison had stepped in beside him.

"It looks like we're heading in the right general direction, maybe off to the west just a little, still."

Alison slid a water bottle from her own pack and pulled a long sip from the nipple before passing it to James. He took a small sip and handed it back. "We probably should conserve this for the trip back. If I'd known we were going out here, I would have brought a few extra bottles."

"Agreed," Alison said. "You think we should keep heading in this direction, or should we start working towards the east a little?"

"I think we're fine. We have a few miles to go before we're even close. With this thick jungle cover, we're not going to be able to see the monument easily."

"Well, we've been walking for what? Ten minutes?"

James glanced at his watch and nodded. "Yeah, about that."

"We're probably hiking at somewhere around two to two and a half miles an hour."

"That sounds about right, considering all the overgrowth we're having to push through. No to mention all the snakes I'm looking out for." James winked.

"Stop! You know I hate snakes." Alison glared at him a moment before continuing. "What I was trying to do was work out our pace so we'll know when we should start turning to the east."

"Yes, yes. Sorry, dear." James snickered and nodded his head.

"Anyway, if we maintain our pace, we should be near the southern structure in about an hour, maybe less. To be safe, we should start looking for signs of ruins in about forty-five minutes."

"Okay. Should we synchronize our watches or ..."

"James." Alison sighed his name. "We're in a foreign jungle, in a restricted area. Can you try and be serious for just a bit?"

James was shocked at Alison's mood shift and nodded silently. He knew she took archeology more seriously than he did, but he was surprised by her sudden loss of humor. He supposed that she was probably just nervous and exhilarated at the same time. He felt the same way and decided to give her a pass.

"Okay. I'll lead on," he said before checking his compass and moving in their original southerly direction.

"I love you, Huggy Bear," Alison said. "This is really the best honeymoon."

James smiled at hearing the pet name that Alison had given him on their third date. "Love you too, babe." He leaned in and kissed Alison before continuing on their trek.

James moved swiftly though the heavily-treed jungle floor. He was surprised at how much more bearable the heat and humidity were now that they were fully immersed in the Mayan jungle. He imagined the tree cover blocking out the sunlight had a lot to do with it. It was still hot, though, as he wiped the sweat from his forehead.

Looking ahead, he visualized a path in their general direction. In order to keep that path, he would have to bob-and-weave a bit around several thickets of trees, but it was nearly passable otherwise.

With their chosen path set, he and Alison

moved in rhythm with one another. Other than the sound of their feet crunching on the jungle floor and the occasional twig snapping as they maneuvered around the trees, there was only silence.

Twenty minutes further into the jungle, they came to a small clearing. It was about a third the size of the one in front of Islaxa, and it appeared to be manmade. The clearing was nearly a perfect circle and there were no established trails leading to or away from it.

"What do you suppose this is all about?" Alison asked as she walked from one edge to the other in a dozen steps.

"Not sure. It looks like machines did it, but how? There are no tracks in or out of the circle, and what happened to the trees?"

James knelt down and ran has hand across the ground. It was worn smooth and there was no sign of vegetation. It was like nothing ever grew there.

"I take that back. This doesn't look manmade at all. It might be ..."

"Don't say it," Alison warned.

"Aliens."

Alison sighed heavily. "It's not aliens."

"Well, what do you think it is? The ground is solid limestone and it's been ground nearly smooth. There's no sign of machinery, so that can only mean aliens." James was only half joking with his wife, but he held a straight face regardless.

"I ... I don't know. Maybe it's a remnant of another Mayan temple, or ..."

"Or aliens."

Alison looked at James and saw something. Something in his eyes that gave it away. "You're an ass sometimes, you know that?"

James grinned. "But I'm a lovable ass."

"Why don't you get your lovable ass up one of these trees and see if the ruins are close."

"Your wish is my command, dear," James said as he scanned the trees on the edge of the clearing.

After passing on the first few trees due to their almost certain inability to hold his weight, he came upon a good-sized Banyan tree that hosted a number of wild vines dropping to the ground. He pulled on a one-inch vine with all his weight and it didn't give. Satisfied, James gripped the vine firmly with both hands and pulled his feet from the ground. Once he was up a few inches, his legs instinctively intertwined with the lowest part of the vine to give him extra support. A small thrust with his legs and he rose another few inches. Hand over hand with small leg pushes in between, and he was halfway to the top in a matter of moments.

"Can you see anything?" Alison asked from below.

James paused his climb long enough to glance toward the upper rim of the canopy. "Not yet. I've got to get higher."

"Be careful," Alison called up, her voice a bit louder than necessary.

James continued his Tarzan-like climb until he reached the point where he felt he would push the limits of the tree's strength. He latched on as best he could, sliding his foot into the V formed where two branches met, and wrapping his arm around the top. He again glanced around, beginning his scan looking due east, slowly drawing his gaze toward the south, and then further to the west. Finally, he saw something.

"It looks like we almost passed it. It looks to be straight that way," James said, pointing his free hand to the west.

"Really? How can that be? I thought we were close, but ..." Alison queried.

Before James responded, he shimmied back down from the thirty foot climb, being careful not to slip from the dampness of his sweating hands. "Yeah, it looks like we almost passed it," he said once his feet met the ground.

"How can that be? I thought we were close to three miles away."

"Your guess, not mine, Babe."

"I don't get it. I thought my distance judging was better than that," Alison continued.

"It's okay. So you misjudged. We could have been moving at a quicker pace too. That could explain some of it."

"Yeah, I suppose you're right."

"Now, that's what I like to hear!" James declared. "Keep that phrase in your mind over the next twenty years or so and we'll get along just fine."

Alison smirked a little before turning on her heel and venturing into the jungle in the direction of the ruin.

"Hey, don't you want me to lead with the compass?" James asked.

Alison just threw a hand in the air and continued to move to the west.

James pulled the compass out and began to follow. His guess had been nearly spot on. The direction they needed to head was precisely west. He slid the compass back into his pocket and trotted to catch up with Alison.

***

Ten minutes later, they stepped out from the jungle and onto a small path that led around the base of an overgrown mound. James could tell there was some sort of manmade structure hiding within the overgrowth, but what it was, exactly, he didn't know.

"From what Arturo said, all the ruins on the site have been covered with jungle growth and appear to be small hills. This one's a big hill," Alison announced.

James didn't say anything as he continued to walk around the base of the jungle-covered mound. As he walked along the trail, he realized that others had to have been there before. Otherwise, why wasn't the trail overgrown as well?

"Well, it doesn't look like we're the first to arrive," he said.

"Eh, it's okay. At least we're here and it is amazing," Alison exclaimed. "Which face of the pyramid do you think is the most accessible?" she asked as they snaked their way around the base.

"Hmm. I don't ... I don't think it's a pyramid," James said, scrutinizing the hilly mound. "It's far too steep to be accessed by foot."

Alison stopped and looked up the slope, trying to compare the incline in her mind to that of the pyramid they had climbed an hour before. "I don't know. It looks the same from my perspective."

James didn't respond because he was nearly twenty feet ahead of her now, and beginning to step out of sight.

"Hey, wait up!" Alison called out and ran to catch up.

James stopped for a moment and glanced up to Alison as she approached. "What do you think is in here?"

He pointed to a separation in the overgrowth that was clearly man-made. Without hesitation, he ducked his head and entered the gap with Alison following close behind. The path through the overgrowth opened up after a few yards. The further they went into the heavy vegetation, the less light shone through from above. James reached back and pulled a flashlight from the side pouch on his backpack. Clicking it on and shining the light forward revealed a plywood panel leaning against a stone wall.

"Well, that doesn't look original. It might have been left from the last remodel," James joked.

"What's behind it?" Alison asked.

"Here. Hold this." James handed her the flashlight before gripping the edges of the plywood and pulling. It didn't move. He looked closely at the edges and it didn't appear to be nailed or screwed. He pulled again, but with more effort. Still no movement.

"Do you need me to get in there and show you how it's done?" Alison asked.

"No, no. I think it's just caught up in all this vegetation."

"Try sliding it to the side."

James tried as Alison suggested, and with a bit of flexing, the panel slid to the right and out of the way. In its place was the outside face of a corbel vault leading beneath the structure.

"Would you look at that. I don't think I've seen an entrance into a pyramid, or any other Mayan structure for that matter, quite like this," James said as he took the flashlight back from Alison and shined it into the pitch-black archway.

"What do you think it is?"

"Hmm. Not sure." James paused as he felt a cool breeze on his face. It smelled earthy to him, but he didn't mind. "The only way to truly find out is to take a look," he said, hesitant to step inside.

"We've come this far. No sense in turning back now," Alison prompted.

Together, they took a step into the vaulted pathway. A moment later, it wasn't wide enough for them to walk side by side, so Alison dropped back a step or two and followed James and the flicker of the flashlight.

"I'm surprised how open and clear the space is," James said, his voice strangely not echoing at all. It was as if the stone walls absorbed his words and muted the ambient sound.

"Whoever covered the entry with plywood must have begun excavation," Alison said as she followed James down the stone tunnel.

The ground was relatively flat for the first few yards into the tunnel. After that, the ground began to slope down at a modest pitch. James slowed his pace and let his free hand glide along the wall to maintain his balance.

James and Alison walked for several minutes, continuing to decline into the bowels of the ancient structure. James stopped several times to shine the flashlight back up the way they had come, but all he saw was darkness beyond the reach of the flashlight beam.

After walking an unknown distance down the declining tunnel, the ground tapered off and became flat once again. James threw the beam of the flashlight ahead and saw the tunnel open up into a room.

"It looks like we're here, wherever this is," he said, stepping into a large, eight-sided chamber. There were tunnel openings on four of the eight walls. The ceiling above was vaulted similar to the tunnels, rising up from each wall and meeting in the middle. James estimated the height to be close to fifteen feet at the center.

As he pored the beam of his flashlight across every inch of the chamber, his eyes came upon four torches mounted on the walls opposite those with tunnel openings.

"Alison, fish out my lighter from my pack, would ya?" he asked as he backed up to her and handed her the flashlight.

Alison unzipped the pack and fumbled around in their gear until she found James's old Zippo and handed it to him.

"Shine that up here," James said as he moved to the first of four torches. He flipped the lid and gently ran his thumb over the rolled striker. The flicker of flame did very little to illuminate the room until the torch caught fire. As he closed his lighter, a gust of wind came through one of the tunnels and blew it out. He repeated the action and lit the torch again. He stood there, lighter in hand, ready to light it a third time if necessary. This time, the torch stayed lit. Satisfied, he moved to the three other torches and lit them as well, each one raising the light level substantially. Alison clicked off the flashlight and tossed it to James to stick back in his pack.

With the room fully lit, James and Alison silently began to take in their surroundings. On four of the walls, ancient hieroglyphs were carved into the stone. James recognized them as Mayan from his studies a few years back, but for the life of him, he couldn't remember any of their translations.

"Can you make any of this out?" James asked.

"A little, but it's been a while since I've studied …" Alison paused.

"Yeah? Studied?" James prompted.

"Did you hear that?" Alison asked.

"Hear what? All I heard was you talking and then stop."

"I could've sworn I heard the voice of a woman speaking …" Alison stepped away from the wall she was near and looked up to James. "Speaking in ancient Mayan dialect."

"Are you sure? When was the last time you heard it actually spoken?" James asked.

"In college, I had a professor who had made the study of the Mayan language her life's work."

"Well, what did the spooky voice say?"

"Hey, don't mock me. I never said it was spooky. And furthermore, I only recognized the language. I have no idea what the words mean."

James recognized Alison's tension rising and knew to back off. He changed the subject.

"What do you think was in the middle of the room here?" he asked, referring to the obvious void in the dirt floor. The void was around four feet by eight feet, and was solid, uninterrupted stone.

"Hmm. That's peculiar. It looks about the size of what the Mayans used as a sacrificial platform, but it could really be anything." Alison paused to slide her foot across the transition of dirt to stone at the edge of the void. When she did so, the top layer of dirt exposed a darker, almost brick colored layer of hardened earth. "That's strange."

"What's that, babe?"

"It looks like dried blood on the floor, but as old as this structure is, it should have degraded a long time ago."

James knelt down and ran his fingers across the darkened ground, picking a chunk off the surface. He raised it to his extended tongue and tasted it.

"Gross!" Alison exclaimed. "You don't know what that is."

"Well, your theory may be correct. It tastes metallic like blood."

"Okay, I know this was all my idea, but this place gives me the creeps. Let's get out of here." Alison begged.

"You must really be spooked. I've never seen you like this before. Let me just take a few pictures of the hieroglyphs first and ..."

"Make it quick," Alison said, cutting James off.

What's gotten into her? James wondered. He dropped the pack off his shoulders and dug in the main compartment for his camera. Pulling it from the bag, he slid the lens cap off and flipped up the attached flash. Not wanting to further irritate Alison, he took three shots of each wall in a matter of moments. After stowing his gear back in the pack, he tossed it over his shoulder and declared, "Okay. Ready."

41

"After you, Huggy Bear."

James smiled at Alison and asked, "I uh ... don't suppose you remember which tunnel we came down, do you?"

"Are you kidding me?" Alison exclaimed. "No, I don't remember. You were leading us the whole way."

James was beginning to feel a little agitated himself, and Alison's anger toward him didn't help. "I'm sorry, dear, but if I'd known you were going to freak out down here, because you thought you heard a voice ..."

"Stop it. I don't want to fight. Can we just get out of here?" Alison begged again.

"It's going to be okay, honey," James said apologetically. "It was probably just the wind or something."

"No, I don't think so. I've been hearing voices nonstop ever since. I ... I just didn't want to say anything." Alison said with concern written across her face.

"Okay, okay. Let's get out of here, then. We'll pick one tunnel and hope for the best. Do you have a preference?"

"Just pick one and let's go."

James turned and headed for the tunnel closest to where he was standing. Before entering the tunnel, he kicked several times at the dirt floor to indicate which one they'd tried first. Entering the tunnel, James glanced about and from his recollection of coming into the chamber, it looked the same. He began the climb up the incline and as he did so, he felt Alison's hand on his lower back. He picked up the pace as safely as possible.

Within minutes, he knew they were in the wrong tunnel, because the ground began to rise more steeply than he remembered. At first, he thought it was his imagination, but as soon as his head started to touch the ceiling he knew.

"We've got to turn around. This is the wrong one."

"Can't we just keep going? I'm sure there's an exit up there."

"I'm sure there is, but the ceiling is already lowering to the point that I have to duck down. Plus, what if there's a plywood barricade up there like the one we found?"

Alison didn't reply. She turned around and began walking back down the descending tunnel in the dark. James did his best to shine the flashlight in front of her until they re-entered the chamber.

Without hesitation, James walked to the tunnel straight across the room, kicked a mark on the floor and entered. Within minutes, he and Alison once again returned to the chamber because of a cave-in fifty feet up the tunnel.

"Well, we have a fifty percent chance this time. Can't get better odds than that, right?"

"Yeah. Sure. Whatever," Alison said, pacing from side to side.

"Do you still hear them? The voices, I mean."

"Yeah, and they're getting louder."

"Can you tell where they're coming from?"

"No, they're just echoing inside my head."

"Alright. Let's try this one," James said as he started for one of the last two tunnel entrances. He clicked on the flashlight and started up the incline. A few minutes into the tunnel, he exclaimed, "Shit! I forgot to mark the tunnel entrance."

"It's okay. I'll go back and do it. I can still see the glow from the torches," Alison said as she turned and jogged down the tunnel.

James leaned against the wall and waited a moment before deciding to follow her down. As he started to walk down the slope, he heard the first of the voices himself. "What?" he asked aloud, instinctively.

There was no response.

"Alison? Are you okay?"

Still no response.

He picked up his pace, and just as he did, he heard Alison scream.

"AAAAIIIIEEEEE!"

"Alison! I'm coming!" James yelped as he sprinted the final twenty feet down the tunnel and into the chamber.

Alison was standing awkwardly in the center of the chamber. Her back was arched inward and her arms were twisted behind her body.

"Babe? Are you okay? You screamed."

"I ... I can't. Move."

James ran to her, and touched her arm. As he did so, he was thrown back against the far wall by some unseen force.

"What the hell!" he exclaimed.

"James. Something has control over me, and I can't move!" Alison yelled. "And the voices are starting ... they're starting to make sense."

"What the hell is going on?" James snapped as he tried to step away from the wall. With every effort he made to move forward, something pushed him back twice as hard. "Don't fight it, Alison. Just try and relax. Let me think for a minute."

"Okay, but hurry up. You do not want to know what the voices are saying."

James was certain of that. He looked around the chamber, and it was vacant, except for him and Alison. The torches burned bright and strong, and nothing seemed different from before.

He moved his head from side to side, and there was no forced resistance to his doing so. He could move his hands and fingers with ease, but when he moved his arms or legs, he felt the pressure exerted against him. Then the voices came. They burst into his mind full force, and although he couldn't understand them, he sensed they weren't friendly.

"Okay, I can't move much at all, and now, I've got your voices. Sorry, babe."

"Same here. It's like I have no control of my own body, and this might sound strange, but I'm starting to get visions."

"Visions?"

"It's like I'm standing here, in this very room, but I'm getting memory flashes that aren't mine. James, I'm scared," Alison said, her voice trembling.

"Dammit!" James exclaimed. He tried to move his arms, but nothing happened. Every effort his mind made was rejected somehow. At least the pressure had stopped.

"Oh, God!" Alison cried.

"What?"

"I can't see. All ... all I can see is this vision."

"What do you see? Tell me."

"I'm standing in this chamber, and there are five men here with me. In the center, there's a big stone block. Oh, God, it's covered with dried blood."

"Alison. Listen to me. Can you close your eyes? Can you fight this?"

"I'm trying, but I can't. It's like I'm meant to see this."

"What are the other men doing? Can you look around in the vision?"

"Um. I can. A little. They're all staring at me. One of the men has his arms strapped behind him. James, my arms are strapped behind my body as well."

James tried with all his might to break free of the possession that had taken hold of him, but it was useless. He couldn't move, and now, his vision was fading to black.

"Oh, no. The room is going dark for me now," he moaned.

"That's how it happened for me. It faded to darkness and then the vision was all I could see. The four other men in the room are dressed in some kind of tribal clothing, with headdresses. Two are standing near the bound man, and two near me. I think they're guards of something. Hold on. They're saying something."

James tried to blink the darkness away, but it was no use. He has lost all control, and was now completely blind. As he continued to blink furiously, images began to form in his mind.

"Hey, I think I'm starting to see something," he said.

A moment later, the vision flashes solidified and he could see the chamber that Alison had described. He could see the four men in the ceremonial clothing and a woman who had her hands tied behind her. He looked down at himself, and he could see that he was confined as well.

"Alison. Can you hear me?"

"I can. James, what do you see?"

"I can see the four men and a woman. She's looking at me right now."

"James, I think we're in the bodies of the two bound people. I can see you looking at me through the man's eyes, but your lips didn't move when you spoke."

James thought for a minute. How else could he see if his wife was in the body of the tied-up woman? He decided to wink and see if she could see that.

"Did you see that?" James asked.

"See what?"

"I just tried to wink. Did you see it?"

Alison said nothing. Instead, the woman's body was forced forward, toward the sacrificial platform. "James!" she shrieked. "I'm moving!"

"I can see, babe. Try not to fight it," James said. All he could do was watch from the edge of the chamber. As the two guards led her to the platform, they began talking in a foreign language.

"What are they saying? Alison?"

"They say that we've been caught having an affair."

James watched and waited. The guard to Alison's left untied her hands and dropped the leather strap to the floor.

"Oh, God. James, they said that our punishment for committing adultery outside of bonding vows is death. First you're supposed to slay me, and then yourself."

The woman's body was laid across the platform and tied at her wrists and ankles. James could see her look in his direction. Then, the two guards standing on either side of him gripped his arms and forced him to the side of the platform. James tried to resist, but his efforts were in vain. He could feel one of the guards remove the binding straps from his wrists and he instantly felt his body lurch toward another guard. A whack on the back of his neck brought a bolt of pain that nearly dropped him to his knees. The guards were saying something, but James could not understand.

"What are they saying?"

"They said that you need to sacrifice me in order for your soul to be let into heaven. I think that's the translation."

"Well, I've got no control here ..." James began, then one of the guards thrust a dagger into his right hand. He looked at it, and knew the hell that was about to come. Instinctively, and not at all by his control, he threw the knife to the ground in protest. A guard picked up the knife and forced it into his hand once again. The guard helped him raise the dagger above his head and pointed it in the direction of the woman's chest. James cried out in protest and tried to release the knife again, but the guard held his hand firmly around James's own. James's only resolve was to follow through with the action.

"Alison, I love you. I'm sorry!" James said as he brought his arm down with full force. As the razor-sharp blade arced toward its target, he felt himself shift its direction slightly and drove it into the thigh of the guard to his right. The guard screamed aloud and released his hold on James's hand. Finally in control of his arms, James pulled the blade from the wound and once again raised it high above his head, the blood of his victim now dripping down his arm.

"Get back!" he yelled. Strangely, he suddenly knew the ancient language as well as he knew his own. The three remaining guards in the chamber did as directed, each backing slowly away, but in a pronounced attack stance. Then, out of their waistbands, they each produced daggers of their own.

With the tables about to turn, James slashed out at them as he stepped closer to Alison. The two guards closest to her saw where he was heading and quickly stepped in between. James lowered his own torso to match theirs, and slashed his knife in their direction. The guard closest to him balked but was able to step aside with ease. The guard closest to Alison redirected his focus from James to her. He turned fully in her direction and raised his dagger above his head and began to mumble.

"STOP!" James screamed, and lunged forward. The guard nearest to him was prepared for the assault and stopped him. James tried to move around, but the third guard had blocked his way. He was trapped. There was nothing he could do but watch the horror unfold.

The guard closest to Alison continued his chant. When James suspected he was nearing the end, he tried once again to circumvent the guards. In his full-force attack, James met the nearest guard with a crack to the bridge of his nose. Blood instantly gushed from the guard's nostrils as he screamed in pain and backed against a wall. James quickly turned his assault to the next guard, but wasn't quick enough. The guard was prepared for the attack and blocked James's assault with his forearm.

Listening to the guard recite the sacrificial incantation, James knew he only had a matter of moments before the dagger was plunged into Alison's chest. He had to make one last effort to save her. He began to yell out a chant of his own – one that had no meaning whatsoever, but it was enough to capture everyone's attention.

James looked into Alison's eyes and saw pure fear. There was no way for her to escape from the woven shackles securing her arms and legs to the enormous stone slab.

As he neared the end of his impromptu chant, the guard hovering over Alison realized it was only a ruse and returned to his own incantation. He suddenly stopped speaking, and James saw him tighten his two-handed grip around the handle of his dagger. He pulled up slightly before beginning its full force drop toward her chest.

"NO!" James screamed and lunged toward Alison. One of the guards reacted quickly, his blade entering James's chest at precisely the same moment the other guard's blade plunged into Alison's.

James staggered back, expecting severe pain, but there was none. The overpowering vision vanished, and he was once again standing in the sacrificial chamber, hovering over Alison. She was lying on a stone slab that hadn't been there before.

"What the hell is this?" James demanded. He tried to step forward but the pressure was back on him, holding him in place.

"I still can't move!" cried Alison.

"Yeah, me neither. I think that vision was just a preview of what's to come."

James glanced down and saw that he was now holding an ancient dagger in his hand – the same one from the vision. It became all too clear what was expected of him. Tears flooded his eyes at the horror of what he was about to do.

"I love you, baby. I am so sorry, but there's nothing I can do to stop this," he said.

She nodded her head, as she also began to cry. "I know. I love you too."

James's body was pushed forward by the unseen forces and as he neared Alison's outstretched body, his arms began to rise above his head.

"Baby, I can't control this. I'm trying, but all I can do is go through the motions. Can you break free?" James asked.

She struggled, but it became clear that she could not. "It's like I'm tied at my wrists and legs, but there's nothing there. I can't move at all."

James's eyes flushed with tears that blurred his vision. He knew the moment was imminent, and his only wish was to see Alison's face clearly once more. He blinked the tears away, and there she was, staring back at him.

I'm so sorry, babe. I wish I could stop this," James sobbed, his hands still raised above Alison.

Alison's tears began to fade, and she closed her eyes. "I love you too, Huggy Bear. I'm ready, and I don't blame you."

James couldn't bear hearing her words of surrender. He tried with all his might to move his body, but he didn't budge.

"I am proud to be your husband," James said as the forces controlling him brought the dagger down and impaled it into Alison's chest. James screamed tears of rage as he did so, and if he hadn't closed his eyes just before the sacrifice, he would have seen the flash of light vacate their bodies as the knife entered Alison's chest.

"Why!" he screamed. "Why her? You could have taken me!"

He dropped to his knees and held Alison's limp hand, once again under his own control. He knelt there, head down, tears streaming from his eyes, each tear dropping into the dry dirt floor.

Suddenly, he felt Alison's hand squeeze his in return, and he jerked his head up. Alison was sitting up and she was smiling down at him.

James looked for the dagger protruding from her chest, but there was none.

"Babe? Are you okay?"

"I am now. Now that I have my own body back."

"But I ... I killed you. What happened?"

"I'm not sure, but right after you stabbed me, I heard more voices. I think they were from the two Mayans who were sacrificed."

"What did they say?"

"They said 'Thank you' and nothing more."

"So that's it? They torture us, and they're on their way?"

"No, I think it was deeper than that. I think maybe ... they couldn't move on from this world until they followed through with a proper sacrifice. We helped them with that, albeit under their control."

"So, it *was* their spirits in our bodies, as we were in theirs earlier?"

"That's my take on it," Alison said as she swung her feet to the floor. "Let's get out of here."

For a moment, James felt like he couldn't move. His head spun from all that had happened over the past few minutes. Then he started to laugh.

"What's so funny?" Alison asked.

"I'm wondering what in the world we're going to tell our friends about all this."

"I ..." Alison started, then stopped. "I don't know."

Still a little shaky, James stood and gave Alison a tender hug. "I love you, babe. Can you – can you forgive me? For what happened?"

"It wasn't you. I know that. I love you too,

Huggy Bear."

Arm in arm, they turned and walked up the tunnel they'd come in through an hour before. James gasped as they stepped out into the heat and humidity of the jungle – then told himself, he'd never felt anything so good in his life. Smiling, he steered his wife back toward civilization.

Afterlife

a Short Story

Paul B Kohler

Wilson Oliver copes with his new reality of dealing with the dead and dying.

I wrote *Afterlife* as a small prequel to Borrowed Souls (available on Amazon), to expand a bit on the character of Wilson Oliver. It is a short scene early in Wilson's career as a Soul Collector.

AFTERLIFE

"Well, don't just stand there, Wilson. You're going to have to give the ol' chap a hand," Hauser said, standing beside his newest pupil.

"But ... he needs to open his mouth, right?" Wilson replied, moving as close to the deceased man as he could bear.

"Yes, but it doesn't look like he's going to give you the assistance you require. You'll have to help him along," snapped Hauser, glancing at his watch. "Anytime, Wilson. We haven't got all day."

Wilson stepped a little closer to the corpse and reached for his mouth. He paused, and pulled back at the last moment. "What did he die from again?"

"It's nothing catching, I promise. Poor fellow was a cancer research volunteer. Unfortunately, his prognosis was grim from the beginning."

"But he looks so ..." Wilson couldn't find the right word.

"Eroded?"

"Yes, that's it. It's like he's been worn from the inside out."

"That's part of the experimental therapy they've been doing here," Hauser said. "Listen, Wilson. Are we going to have a problem with this? Because if we are, you might put in for a relocation. The research facility here at Berkeley has a fairly low mortality rate. If you're going to get squeamish with every dead body you come across, perhaps–"

"No, no. I can do this. It's just ... going to take a little getting used to, is all," Wilson assured his mentor. Staring at the cadaver, he wondered if he had made the wrong choice when his own soul was being collected. If he had known how gruesome the job was going to be, he might have let his soul be captured without protest. But, as chance sometimes has it, the doctors were able to miraculously restart his heart after 43 minutes – just long enough to send out the collector.

As Wilson stood motionless, he remembered every moment of the last two weeks with extreme clarity. He had met some nice people, as well as some not so nice people in their final moments. With each soul he collected, he felt that he had learned a little something... and with that newfound knowledge, he discovered that the job became even harder. In addition to his own problems, he was burdened with the ones that had been shared with him.

Now, standing in front of a man who had been ravaged by disease, Wilson felt like he had a decision to make. Should he tell Hauser how he felt or continue on, hoping against hope that the job would get easier over time?

"Wilson? Are you there?" asked Hauser.

"Yes, yes. I was just thinking about ... oh, it was nothing."

He once again reached forward and forced open the lower jaw of the cadaver. Once the mouth was open as far as Wilson could get it, he fumbled in his pocket for the wooden box he had received after his last capture. Wilson nearly dropped the box to the floor before Hauser spoke.

"Easy, Wilson. It's not a race. Just relax."

Easy for you to say, Wilson thought as he

managed to turn the box around so he could see the name engraved across the lid. "Jason Porter. How do you do?" Wilson asked the dead man. Unsurprisingly, he received no reply.

Wilson flipped the brass latch, opened the box and sat it on the chest of the corpse. "This is the first one that's been really dead. How long ..."

"It'll be quick. The soul knows what to do," Hauser said, motioning to the body.

As he did, a small wisp of smoke began to slip from Jason Porter's open mouth. It rose above the gurney, nearly reaching the suspended light fixture before it arched its way into the open box.

Once the smoke was fully in the box, Wilson snapped it closed and fastened the latch. No sooner did he have it closed, than the box vanished from his hands.

"Well, now. How many does that make for you?" asked Hauser.

"Including my own replacement soul, that made nineteen," Wilson replied, looking glum.

"Why the long face? It's just a job, you know," Hauser said.

"I suppose. It's just that I was getting used to speaking with the dead before taking their souls. Why wasn't that possible with

Jason?" Wilson asked.

"Something to do with the cancer. Jason had smoked for far too many years to know any better, and his lungs were shot. Trust me on this one – it was better this way." Hauser paused and glanced around the sterile facility. "Many years ago, I was training another soul collector, and the man that passed on had nearly been severed in half in a mining accident. It was so bad, he whistled when he talked."

"You mean like a rasp?" asked Wilson.

"No, not quite. Let's just say that the air to fill his lungs didn't come through his mouth," Hauser said with a wink.

"Oh. Oh, dear," Wilson said.

"Now. Your next box should be along shortly. Until then, what do you say we head over to Fisherman's Wharf and watch the ships come in?"

Wilson nodded. He'd begun to walk towards the door when Hauser grasped his arm and said, "Come now, Wilson. You'll have to adjust to your new life. Walking from place to place takes far too much time. Use the gifts bestowed upon you. Your afterlife will be much more rewarding if you do."

Wilson looked into Hauser's dark eyes just as he winked and vanished.

"Dammit, Hauser!" Wilson said before closing his eyes and quickly imagining the wharf in his mind.

A moment later, he too vanished from the cancer research facility.

ALONE

A SHORT STORY

PAUL B KOHLER

A sleepless night forces Rob McArthur to question what is causing him to lose sleep, life, and whether he's alone in his feelings.

Alone is a short story I wrote 10 years ago. Although this story isn't packed full of action, I feel that many people can relate to in some way. I submitted it to be included in Something to Take on the Trip - A Charity Anthology. It was accepted and published in March of 2014.

ALONE

It was the time of night where staying up too late danced with being up too early. Rob McArthur couldn't sleep. He lay there, awake in bed, thoughts invading his rest until slumber was a lost cause. He tried to close his eyes, but they remained open, staring into the dark void of night. He glanced from dark spot to dark spot, visualizing what each shadow was. When his eyes wandered toward the window, all he could see was the same bleakness.

If he couldn't sleep, then he might as well get up, he thought. He rolled from bed and fumbled for something to cover his body. His sweatpants would do. He was just going to go down to the kitchen, maybe have a snack or find a warm glass of milk.

He found his sweats at the foot of the bed and quietly pulled them on. His wife had no problems with sleep this night, and Rob didn't want to wake her. He stood back up and walked toward the window. His eyes were now fully adjusted to the dark, and he noticed the only visible star in the sky. How glorious it was to illuminate so much of his earth with such small vastness. He looked up and down the street, expecting to see a car or someone walking alone, but it was empty. He looked across the street to Ted's house. All dark. He had hoped that he wasn't up alone on this sleepless night.

He slipped out into the hallway and down the stairs, deftly maneuvering without turning on a single light. This was the third time this week that Rob was up looking for something to put him back to sleep. He was overwhelmed by the uncontrollable rush of thoughts. He tried to pinpoint which of the thoughts that kept him awake, but there were too many. To isolate just one was madness, so he gave in to them. Night after night he gave in. Never changing.

The glow of the clock on the stove showed him that it was just past four o'clock in the morning.

"What am I doing?" he mumbled aloud in hopes that someone might actually be there to answer him. There was no answer. The only thing he heard was the light breeze outside knocking upon the windows. He moved toward the window over the sink and looked out. He saw the same darkness that he had seen from his bedroom window. He continued to stare out into the nothingness for what felt like an eternity, never fixating on any one thing. He finally moved from there and opened the fridge. He pulled out the milk and poured a half-full glass to be warmed in the microwave. Thirty seconds should do the trick, he thought as he pushed start. The whine of the machine broke the silence of night, and the light shone on his tired face. Oh yes, he was tired. Maybe too tired to sleep.

BEEP. BEEP. BEEP.

He pulled the warm glass from the microwave and sat at the kitchen table sipping it like a glass of brandy. He sat there in silence while his mind raced from thought to thought. He knew if he were to continue at that pace he would someday give himself a stroke.

He finished the glass of milk and left it sitting on the table. He was staring outside again. Why was it that when he was up late at night, he fixated on staring outside? Why not stare at the floor or the ceiling? No. He always stared outside. Did everyone else stare outside like this when they were up at 4:00 a.m.? Most likely not. They were all sleeping. He was in this alone. He knew it. But why did he have to be? Why couldn't there be someone else here with him?

He pushed the thoughts from his mind and moved toward the backdoor. He opened it and stepped through into the coolness of night. It was mid-June and everything was in bloom. He could smell the faint fragrances in the breeze. He slumped down into a patio chair and stared up to the stars. There were lots of them now. From his bedroom he had only been able to see one, toward the north, but now there were hundreds of them. Probably thousands. Rob stared at one, wondering if it would move if he stared at it long enough. When it didn't, he looked at the next one and then the next. Each time his eyes moved to another star, the last one appeared to move. He knew it was his mind playing tricks on him, so he resisted looking back.

He gazed at the stars for a long time. He wondered if there was actually life out there.

He often wondered if people on this planet were alone. He was alone. But only in the simple sense that nobody was around for him to talk to or even just to be with.

Rob had married the first woman that would go out with him. He sometimes knew this was a mistake, but he loved her nonetheless. He was just not in love with her. There was no spark there anymore. It had moved out years ago. Rob pushed the thoughts from his mind and again focused on the stars. When he noticed the faint glow from the horizon, he decided to return to bed and attempt sleep once again.

He retraced his steps back inside, back upstairs, and then back into his bedroom. He slipped out of his clothes and slid back into bed. It all took less than a minute, and soon he was fast asleep, only to be woken by his alarm an hour later.

GOLD

EST 2014

RUSH

A SHORT STORY

BY PAUL B KOHLER

A futuristic glimpse of an age old era that time has forgotten.

A futuristic glimpse of an age old era that time has forgotten.

Gold Rush was a flash fiction story I wrote for an online competition in 2013. It won the competition and has gone on to be included in Something for the Journey - A Charity Anthology, which published in November of 2013.

GOLD RUSH

The man across the table was a codger with greying hair and sideburns to match. His stern look said everything that it should about the times and lives of his ancestors. He sat resolutely, as if waiting for the purpose of life to be revealed presently. He wore a faded and tattered outfit that contributed to the illusion of having stepped out of the old west. All that was missing was the token Panama hat covered in dust.

Had he known just how foolish he looked, he might have opted to at least smile knowingly. But DeWitt, as his equally faded nametag read, was playing the role precisely. He was the quintessential gold miner.

"Come again?" I asked.

"It's called the new gold rush, son," said the old man with strong indignation.

"I thought that's what you said. I wanted to be sure before I, um . . ." I stopped speaking when I noticed DeWitt appear to become more agitated.

"Before you what?" he snapped.

Honestly not wanting to offend the old man, I smiled nervously before replying. "Where do I sign up?"

DeWitt produced a sheath of papers attached to an antique clip board and shoved them into my hands. "Fill 'em out. Next tour begins in twenty minutes."

He returned to his desk as I sat across the room, as far from earshot as possible. I began to thumb through the paperwork. I soon realized that this was not really a "new gold rush," as DeWitt put it, but an exploitation of the historic time period. When the famed chemist Dr. Rasmus duplicated the chemical composition of gold in a lab in 2125, the precious metal lost most of its value. I chuckled and continued to complete the forms as requested. Actually filling out paperwork, with paper and pen was quirky. I couldn't remember the last time "paperwork" wasn't completed on one of the latest transparent data-tablets, and signed on the dotted line with a mere thumbprint.

As I signed the last of the numerous waivers and releases, I glanced up and noticed the room had filled with many other visitors, all of them equally fascinated at the thought of an actual gold mine tour taking place in the twenty-second century. Time had moved on from the past so much so that in the bustle of city life, age and wisdom were relics in an era of newness and youth. Even in history classes, not a whole lot was taught of that time when greed and lust ruled the land. Now, what ruled the land was technology in a minimalistic culture.

Had I not have traveled hundreds of kilometers to see this place with my own eyes, for a school assignment no less, I would have most certainly turned back. But as I was already here, I was going to follow through with the ridiculous task of reviewing this nostalgic enigma of the Wild West. "It's called the new gold rush, son," resonated in my mind, and I uncontrollably chuckled at the irony of the old man's superior attitude coupled with his laughable attire. DeWitt seemed to know what I was thinking; he glared wickedly at me from across the now-filled room.

I stood up and negotiated my way

through the crowd over to his desk. I slid the completed paperwork across his desk and waited silently. He snatched it up and flipped through it, nodding in approval at each sheet. When he reached the end, he tossed it aside and looked up at me.

"Now alls I need is yer admission fee."

"How much?"

"Well, that all depends, son. Do you want the full guided tour with all the bells and whistles, or do you want the bare bones tour with just a map and a flashlight?"

"Have anything in between?" I asked.

"Nope. One or the other. But I have to say, it's not a big savings for the bare bones tour."

"Then I guess I'll take the full tour."

"That'll be $3,975. Just one, right?"

This guy expected me to blow a full month's rent to walk through a run-down gold mine? "Come again?" I asked.

"Are you hard of hearin', son? That's three thousand, nine hundred and seventy-five dollars." DeWitt was the cranky old codger to the end.

It was at that very point that I realized just what the New Gold Rush was all about. I thought for a moment before replying.

"I'll just take the bare bones tour." And I

handed him my expense card.

PAUL B. KOHLER

LOOKOUT MOUNTAIN

A Short Story

Depression nearly gets the best of Ian, but his mind saves him before he firmly hits the ground.

Lookout Mountain was a short story - flash fiction, really - that I wrote several years ago. I was experimenting with the mental aspects of suicide. I submitted it to be included in Something for the Journey - A Charity Anthology, and it was accepted and published in November of 2013.

LOOKOUT MOUNTAIN

Ian Bradley began the ascent to his demise. He knew he was doing the right thing, and it would all be over soon enough. Still, he felt more overwhelmed than ever.

With each step on the dusty trail that led up the mountainside, Ian's feelings of self-pity grew. He regretted not living his life to the fullest. He had never taken his wife on the trip he'd promised. He had completely forgotten about his daughter's last choir concert. He hadn't even been able to finish high school. Everyone has regrets, but Ian's failures overwhelmed him. He picked up his pace.

The tree branches hung low over the trail,

and he had to duck his head to avoid them brushing at his face.

Ian thought about everything that was wrong, and it all made him more distraught. How could he have let things get so out of control? He wanted it all to end. He wanted it all to go away.

He was broke. So broke, he had to borrow money for gas to drive up the mountain. His parents didn't handle money matters well either, and all his life he told himself that he would never follow in their footsteps. When did it all change? Here he was, thirty-three and in a dead end job.

Bill collectors called his house nonstop, just as they had called his parents while he was growing up. Nothing stood out more in his mind than having to lie over the phone about his parents not being home. He lied even as they stood next to him.

Aside from his financial problems, which were a mountain in themselves, Ian knew that nobody liked him. When his wife's car had been repossessed, he had seen Bob and Eve across the street whispering to each other. His coworkers always stopped talking when he walked in the room. He knew with conviction that his boss hated him.

Ian brushed the tree branches from his

view and saw the top of the mountain a few hundred feet away. How was he going to do it? Get to the top and just step off? Or was a running jump better? He had no idea. All he knew was it was all going to end shortly, and for that he was thankful.

The irony of being thankful for something so morose sickened him, so he pushed the thought from his mind. In its place popped the memory of the car being repossessed. Seeing the tow truck driving off with the car chained behind it had made his soul ache. Sure, the car was just a materialistic thing, but what was next? A house foreclosure? A divorce? He didn't want to be around to find out. And the worst part was that he had nobody to blame but himself. It was all his fault.

Over the last month, the thoughts of this very day had raced through his mind. One day he considered putting a bullet to his temple on one day, the next he thought of jumping in front of a train. Regardless of the method, the result would be the same: the end of it all. It was best for everyone. His life insurance was paid up, and the thought of setting everything right by his death made him feel a little better. He vacillated about whether to leave a note or not, but in the end no note was written. He was certain nobody would miss him.

After every imagined suicide, Ian's mind would turn to the memorial. He imagined floating above the small crowd of people, listening to each of them speak nice things about him. Then he would realize that none of his friends or relatives were there. Did they dislike him so much that they wouldn't honor his death by at least attending his memorial?

Every time he thought about it, he ended up with the same conclusion—he was a hated man. But soon, everything would be different. Once he was gone, he knew that they would all feel differently. They would all regret not knowing him better.

Feeling like he had already won, he stepped out from the cover of trees and proceeded to the edge of the cliff. There he was, on top of Lookout Mountain, finally in full control of his destiny. The path was not as he intended, but he was in full control nonetheless.

He had been just a boy when his Scout troop came to this area to do cleanup. Ian and his best friend, David, were supposed to be bagging trash, but they were playing a bravery game instead. The game was to see who could walk the longest along the edge of the cliff. The game looked to be a stalemate when, suddenly, David lost his footing and fell. The fall was quick, and David was gone in an instant. From that day, Ian felt that this place would play in important part in his own life, but he had no idea how. Until now.

Ian took in a breath of fresh mountain air as he looked around. He could see for miles in every direction. He thought he would be able to see the nearest mountain town, nestled in the valley, but all he saw were tree tops and a sky so blue and bright, Ian had to squint. It was beautiful. The thought of dying in such a beautiful place put him more at ease than he would have ever thought possible.

He had imagined that he would get up here and change his mind. He thought he would back down like a coward. But not this time. This was the right thing to do.

He took one last glimpse of his surroundings and then looked straight down. He took a few deep breaths and he knew he was ready. The thoughts of all the bad things in his life almost pushed him over the edge. But Ian didn't need pushing now. He was his own man, in full control of his destiny. He closed his eyes and stepped off the edge.

The instant the earth beneath his feet

was gone, he experienced a happiness that he had not felt in a long time; a euphoria calmed his senses. The feeling, however, only lasted a moment. He quickly realized his mistake. He had never once thought about the good in his life.

Ian's surroundings, his whole life, slowed to a crawl. His mind raced to and from all things positive. The single happiest thought was of his daughter, so beautiful and innocent, so unknowing. Then the memory of his wife flashed in. Despite their problems, she had stayed with him. How had he missed seeing that? Thoughts of his mother and in-laws came next. Then his friend Kurt. Kate, who sat across from him at work and always had a smile for him. Even Bob and Eve, who had invited them over for dinner at least once a week.

Ian was falling to his death. He could see the rocky mountainside pass by him in great detail and realized that he would never see the beautiful surroundings again. The smell of fresh pine needles filled his nose, and the scent drew tears to his eyes. He knew that he had made a tremendous error in judgment. There was so much more to live for than there was to die for. He wanted to take it back.

He tried to grasp at something to stop his fall, but it was far too late. The bottom was coming ever closer, and what he truly loved and cherished was slipping further and further away. His heart beat faster the closer he got to earth. Beads of sweat instantly materialized as he began to shake and grasp at anything he could. He wanted to live. He wanted to love. He wanted to go back to what he was.

"WAIT!" he screamed, but nobody could hear him.

The bottom of his fall was coming faster now, and he knew the end was nigh. He expected to feel an instant of excruciating misery before he died, but he felt nothing of the sort. He opened his eyes. He was still standing at the top of Lookout Mountain.

The sudden realization caused Ian to weep. Tears of happiness instead of dread. He had made the climb to end his life, but in that moment, Ian Bradley was reborn.

linear
shift.

PART ONE

No one said time travel would be easy.

Peter Cooper, a widowed father of two whose life is crumbling around him—until a bizarre encounter with a desperate Army general launches him on a risky mission: to go back to 1942 and change a moment in time. The repercussions will almost certainly alter the conclusion of World War II. But will the ripple effects stop there? And what kind of life will Peter return to?

Linear Shift, Part 1 is the first part to a serialized novel. It was written and published in September of 2013. Part 2 was written and published in December of 2013. The third, and final part, is currently being written.

LINEAR SHIFT, PART 1

CHAPTER 0
February 11th, 1942

Dr. Bernard Epson sat triumphantly in his studio laboratory, applying the final touches to his theory of time travel. It had been twelve grueling years since he'd first begun his groundbreaking project. Completion was near, and his tongue could taste the finality, like the tang of history itself. He leaned back in his worn leather chair, basking in his accomplishment, his eyes surveying the notes and scribblings placed on virtually every surface in his modest workshop.

Bernard dreaded his next exercise. With

the majority of his progressive research documented in his journals, this final stage was troublesome but necessary. The creak of the front door redirected his attention to the man entering his lab.

"Professor? Good morning. Have you been here long?" asked his assistant as he closed the oil-starved door behind him.

"Wha? Oh yes. I, um... I haven't been home yet. Is it really morning?" he replied drearily, longing someday for a workspace with a window. He'd lost count of how many sleepless nights he had spent in his lab alone.

"Yes, Professor. It's just after seven." he paused as he crossed to his diminutive desk in the corner of the room. "You promised me that you wouldn't work yourself so hard. Have you eaten?"

"Um, yes. I had Miss Stewart bring me a *croque-monsieur* before she left last night," lied the doctor. As the words escaped his mouth, he realized he was famished.

"Well, that's good, sir. Did you make any progress on the final equations?" he inquired with abundant interest.

"As a matter of fact, I resolved the final hurdle not fifteen minutes ago." Dr. Epson sprang from his chair, ignoring the protests from his fatigued muscles. "You see, if we replace this algorithm with..."

As Dr. Epson continued with his explanation, his assistant listened intently, masking his concerns. As a member of the *Society,* he, like his associates, prayed the professor would never unlock the secrets to time travel. The professor's successes were a complication that required subtle interference. Only half-listening to the doctor's commentary, his mind began to devise a way to sidetrack the man's progress. He needed to get the doctor out of the lab for a while, so that he could alter a few of the minute, yet critical calculations before they could be recorded.

"That's fantastic, Professor! You must be extremely proud of this monumental achievement." His compliment was genuine, but not entirely sincere. "I think what we need is a celebration. You've been here all night and must be exhausted. Why don't you go home and catch a quick nap? After you're rested, we can go out for a celebratory lunch. It'll be my treat—and afterward, we can begin the process of recording all of your data into the journals."

Bernard was tired and knew that if he began the tedious task of documenting the observations now, he would make mistakes. What his trusted assistant suggested was wise.

"All right. I accept your offer of celebration. Let's make it three and invite Miss Stewart." Dr. Epson hoped his affection for the attractive Miss Stewart would not canvas his face. She had been in his employ from the very beginning, and although they had worked together for years, he had never yet found the courage to act upon his feelings.

"I think that is a wonderful idea, Professor. I'll set everything up. You go and get some rest." He nearly shoved the doctor towards his coat.

"Yes, yes. I'll get some rest, but as soon as we're back from lunch, we'll get this recorded and begin staging the build. I want to test this device by mid-year!"

His assistant was staggered. "You want to what?" he stammered.

"I want to start testing the device within the next four months."

'But—but how can we do that without funding?"

"Oh come now, my boy. Do you think I haven't been dreaming of this day for years? I have more than enough money to build the first device, and I know that once it's complete, I'll be able to persuade someone to invest in the future. Or the past, as it were." He chuckled.

Dr. Bernard Epson's devious assistant was speechless. He'd have to act more swiftly than he'd anticipated in order to keep the doctor from moving the project to the next stage. With subterfuge on his mind, he smiled brightly. "Fantastic, sir! I can't wait to assist you in this historical undertaking!"

The doctor donned his topcoat and hat and bid his assistant a brief farewell. As he walked out the door, he began to eagerly ponder what his first time travel destination would be.

CHAPTER 1
Present day

The sign on the door read "NOTICE OF EVICTION"—it was unmistakable. Peter was at a loss for words, despite having known it was coming. He stood there, staring at the notice as if waiting for the words to mysteriously change before his eyes. They did not. Peter pulled the attached document from his entry door and read it thoroughly.

Disgusted, he folded the notice in half and unlocked the door before going inside, just like he had done thousands of times before. *This is my house, dammit! You'd think unemployed folks could get a break!* These thoughts flooded his mind as he mindlessly dropped his keys on the table in the foyer and walked into his study, ignoring the pile of mail on the floor.

The lights were out and the wooden

shutters were closed tight. It was dark, just the way Peter liked it in his study. He crossed the room, clicked on his Tiffany-styled desk lamp and fell into his tufted leather chair. He was still holding the eviction notice and he read it once more for clarity. He *was* going to lose the house. He felt like he was losing everything. First his wife, two years ago, then his job a year ago, and now the house. Pretty shitty three-year run. It wasn't even the house itself that Peter felt so attached to, so much as the fact that it was the first purchase he'd made with Minnie after getting married. He believed they would grow old and die in this house. Peter closed his eyes, and wondered where it had all gone wrong. He thought he was a good husband. Hell, he *was* a good husband, but that didn't matter to the drunk driver that stole his wife. He thought he was a good employee. He was, but that didn't matter when the economy hit the skids and he was laid off. He knew he was responsible with his finances, but without a job, and without a secondary income, his savings could only go so far.

He leaned forward, scanned the papers strewn across his desk, and placed the eviction notice in the appropriate pile: delinquent. The unfortunate thing about the piles on his desk was that they were *all* delinquent bills, and the house payment being ninety days behind trumped them all. He was screwed, and he knew it.

Leaning back with his eyes closed, he thought back to the first time he'd walked into the 1940's-era French Eclectic, hand-in-hand with Minnie. It had been such an exciting time for them. Having married earlier that year, and then finding out that she was expecting their first child, they both realized that starting a family in a small, two-bedroom brownstone wasn't ideal. They made the decision to move out of the city and into the suburbs. Their broker found an old provincial in desperate need of repair. With a fixer-upper, there was a deal to be had, and Peter was right for the job. He had recently completed his first internship with a well-known architecture firm and was applying for his registration. His strong knack for design and construction made the remodel a perfect fit. He and Minnie had walked from room to room, imagining the potential each possessed. Every nook and cranny of the house seemed to have a story of its own, and they talked about all the future memories they could create.

The house was old and had a lot of

character. The floorboards squeaked. The doors stuck. Several light switches did nothing that they knew of. It was perfect. They closed on the house some forty days later, and immediately started remodel work. Floor by floor, room by room, they stripped paint and sanded floors. Their plan was to get the baby's room done first, and then work from the far side of the house inward, so the noise would be far enough from Tori's room that they could work during nap times. Within eighteen months, they had finished the remodel. And with timing bordering on perfection, Minnie was then pregnant with their second child.

Peter forced the memories from his mind. He knew that dwelling on the past would make moving so much harder. Where did he go wrong? What karma had caused him to have such bad luck? He'd asked himself those questions every day since Minnie was killed by that drunken bastard. If she could have been just a few minutes early or late, she would still be there with him, and everything would be all right. But she wasn't. She was always on time, and time was not kind to Minnie.

Peter straightened himself in his chair and glanced at the clock. It was 2:45 on a

Wednesday. He wiped the tears from his eyes and walked out of his study. He didn't want the kids to see him like that and they would be coming home from school shortly.

CHAPTER 2

Peter sat in the cluttered living room, patiently listening to his fifteen-year-old daughter explain the multitude of reasons why she should have her nose pierced.

"Please, Dad?" Tori begged. "All my friends have theirs pierced... Becca even got her tongue pierced!"

"Tori, I don't care how many of your friends have piercings, or what parts of their bodies are pierced. You're not getting it done. When you turn eighteen, you can put as many holes in your body as you want." Peter sighed. "Until then, no holes."

"What about my ears, Dad? *They* have holes!" Tori pulled the long black hair away from her face and thrust one ear toward her dad.

Peter looked up and winced ever so slightly. He could never get used to the idea that Tori had chosen to dye her beautiful, naturally blond hair a solid jet black.

"Ears are different, Tori, and you know it. We've talked about this before, and you know where I stand on all the 'body art' that goes on these days." Peter used his fingers to make air quotes when he said 'body art.' He had an affinity for air quotes. "I will not have a child of mine, who lives under my roof, have any of that crap."

Tori sat in silence and glared at her father. She knew now that she should have listened to Becca. Becca had told her that her dad would never agree to it, and that she should just get it done. "It's better to ask for forgiveness than permission," she'd said. "The worst that could happen is you get grounded. And after that, you'll have your nose pierced!" Becca's words had rattled inside her head all afternoon.

"Mom would have let me get it done," Tori blurted out after several moments of silence. The words were out of her mouth before she could pull them back. The look on her dad's face was indescribable. He still found it hard to even hear her name without breaking down.

"Well, mom is not here, and I'm done talking about this."

"Well, I'm not!" shouted Tori. She said it

loudly enough that her brother Brett opened his bedroom door and peeked out, but nobody noticed. "I'm fifteen years old, Dad. I get my license in eight months. You keep telling me that I'll have so much responsibility then. Why not let this happen now?"

Peter glared at his daughter with that look that only a single father can muster, then walked into the kitchen. Tori didn't follow.

As Peter started making dinner, his mind replayed their argument. He wondered if he had been right to be so firm with Tori. He seemed to be asking that question of himself more and more lately. Ever since his Minnie had died, both of the kids had pulled away. And to a certain extent, he felt they resented him—simply because it wasn't him that had died in the car crash. Neither of them had come out and said it, but Peter could feel the truth by the way they both looked and reacted toward him.

After standing in front of an open fridge for far too long, he pushed the thoughts from his mind and returned to making dinner.

* * *

Conversation at the dinner table was practically nonexistent. Tori barely touched the spaghetti. She just sat in her chair, sulking and pushing her food from one side of her plate to the other.

Brett, on the other hand, had no problems eating. He scarfed in silence, and as he neared the bottom of his plate, he just as silently stood to clear his place. Not a single word by either of them.

Peter was okay with the silence. As tense as he and Tori had been an hour earlier, he knew it was best for everyone to simmer down a bit.

CHAPTER 3

Peter guided his newly acquired minivan into the parent parking lot of Willow Canyon High School and found a vacant space in the second row. Turning off the engine, he reached over to the passenger seat and picked up the manila folder filled with the dealership documents. With teary eyes, he opened the folder and flipped through the sales forms for his trade-in. His Mercedes had been a conduit to his old life. It had been an anniversary gift. He knew that trading down to the 1995 Chevy Astro was the logical thing to do; it seemed to be the cheapest yet most reliable ride on the lot. And the residual cash would aid in finding a new home. The mortgage payments and late fees were far beyond this meager sum, but it should at least be enough for a security deposit on an economy apartment across town.

Tossing the folder and contracts onto the

console, Peter glanced at his watch. He was early. He had expected the negotiation at the dealer to take much longer than it did, but arriving at the school early gave him time to assess how he would tell the kids that they would be moving.

Over the past few weeks, he'd rehearsed the conversation in his mind. He'd ultimately known this day was coming, and he loathed himself for not having been able to avoid it. He knew that Tori would be devastated by the news, but also knew that Brett would go with the flow. He wished Tori could be more like Brett. Why did she have to be so much like her mother? Damn, he missed Minnie.

Moments later, teenagers began to pour out of the school exits. Peter had decided that today was the day for "the talk." Brett would probably be out first, and Tori would amble out a few minutes later. Knowing they wouldn't recognize the turquoise POS, instead of the crimson S-class, he climbed out and walked over to the sidewalk. He leaned against a light pole to wait.

It wasn't long before Brett walked up with a confused look on his face.

"How was your day, buddy?"

"Okay, I guess. Whatta ya doing here?" he replied, looking around for the car.

Peter noticed, smiled as best he could, and said, "I've got some news. We should wait until Tori comes out and we'll talk about it."

Brett nodded and stood uncomfortably to Peter's side. Tori came out a few minutes later with a few friends, and when they got closer, she whispered to them and they redirected without breaking stride. She looked up to her dad nervously. "What's going on, Dad?"

He loved and hated how smart she was. She knew something was coming... "I've got some news. Let's go somewhere where we can sit and chat."

Peter grabbed Tori's backpack and led the way. As they approached the van, Peter exclaimed—in his most chipper tone—"I traded in the Mercedes today. What do you think?"

Brett was silent, as always, but Tori was never one to hold her tongue. "I think it sucks! I can't believe you're picking us up in this. Where's the car?"

Inside, Peter hurt. Outside, he clowned. "Oh, come on, Tori. Don't you like the color? It's kind of funky, don't you think? This *is* the car!"

"Barf, whatever..." is all she muttered as she climbed into the passenger seat.

"How about we go for some ice cream? It's a warm day, and two scoops would hit the spot," Peter said, trying to make the best of the situation. Neither kid answered. "Okay. Ice cream it is."

Peter pulled the minivan out of the parking lot and headed toward the nearest ice cream shop. Thankfully, Geno's Gelatos was not three blocks from the school. He pulled off the street and into a parking spot near the entrance. Just as he turned off the engine, Tori looked over at her dad and asked, "What's going on, Dad? This is all too weird."

Before Peter answered, he glanced back in the mirror to see if Brett was paying attention. He was staring idly out the side window, but looked up a moment later.

"Well... I've got some bad news. Because I've been unemployed for so long, the house payments have gotten behind. There's no way for me to get caught up, and the bank has exhausted their patience. We're going to have to move."

As he said it, he looked at each of the kids. Brett was looking outside again, while Tori stared straight ahead. Neither of them said anything. Peter continued to watch them in silence, and it wasn't long before Tori began to cry. He couldn't tell how Brett was handling what he'd just said, because Brett's attention appeared to be focused elsewhere. Peter followed Brett's gaze and his eyes landed on a couple passing the van. It was obvious why his son was so enthralled with the couple. The woman gave him goosebumps. She was stunning, around five-foot-six, with long, vibrant brunette hair. She was very athletic and had a regal bearing. That's when Peter noticed the man she was with. He seemed ridiculously mismatched to the woman: he was six-six, thick without being portly, with a receding hairline and a pockmarked face.

While watching the two walk into the ice cream shop, he momentarily forgot about the bad news. His heart ached. Snapping back to the moment, he once again glanced at Tori. She had wiped the tears away from her cheeks as the rage built in her face. *Here it comes*, Peter thought.

"Can't you get a loan or something? I'm a sophomore in high school, Dad! It's hard enough making friends here! I cannot start over at another school!"

Peter tried to keep his voice calm and positive. "I'm not so sure we would have to change schools. If I can find a place we can afford for a while, we might be able to keep you both here." Peter wished that what he was saying *could* be true—but in reality, he knew they would have to change schools. Their current neighborhood was fairly upscale, and there was no economy housing in the area.

"When are we going to have to leave?"

"I don't know, Tori. The notice came yesterday. They usually give three to four days on something like this. First off, we can put most of our stuff in storage until we can find a place. We'll probably need to stay at a motel for a week or so."

"A motel?! Seriously?! Dad!"

"Listen, Tori." Peter didn't mean to snap, but he did. "It's not like I planned for this to happen. I want to stay in the house as much as you do. But, this is how it is. I sold the Mercedes to help with money for now. I'm really trying to do my best here."

Tori began to sob. Looking back at Brett, Peter saw that now he was crying too. Seeing both of his children in tears, Peter began to cry, too. He wanted to be strong—*needed* to be strong for the kids, but it was so damn hard. He hurt deeply for letting them down and there was nothing he could do to make things right.

"Let's go in and get some ice cream,"

Peter said finally, wiping his own tears away. Brett was already out of the car heading for the door before Tori unlatched her seat belt. "Listen, kiddo. Please believe me when I say this. I love you both and I want only the best for you. If I could make things right, you know I would."

She relented. "I know, Dad. But what will all my friends think?"

'Well, they shouldn't give it a second thought if they're real friends. I promise you, Tori. I will do everything possible not to interrupt your high school experience. If I have to drive you back and forth to school forty-five minutes each way, then that's what I'll do."

Tori sat in silence a few moments longer. Brett still stood just outside the shop, staring inside at the couple that had walked in moments earlier.

"Okay, Dad. I'll do my best to stay positive."

"Thanks, kiddo." Peter hugged her warmly. "Let's go, before Brett adopts that other couple as his parents." Tori chuckled lightly, and that was the first time in ages he had seen her smile.

CHAPTER 4

The knock on the door was loud enough to be heard in the basement, where Peter was going through some old boxes. He was trying to make some headway before they had to move. Another knock, more insistent this time.

"Dammit," he exclaimed aloud, even though only the dust heard him. Ascending the stairs two at a time, he swiftly made his way to the front door. Just as he reached for the door handle, the loud knock came again. Peter yanked the door open and, without thinking, blurted out, "Enough already!"

"Hello. I'm looking for Mr. Peter Cooper?" said the man at the door. To Peter's surprise, the man was wearing a U.S. Army brigadier general's uniform. Peter recognized it right away, from his days in the service.

"I'm Peter," he said, looking around the general to see if he had any more company.

"Not to worry, Mr. Cooper. There is nothing wrong. I'm here on somewhat of a private matter. May I have a few moments of your time?"

Peter stood there for a moment, wondering what a general from the army would want with him. His mind flashed back to the days prior to his enlisting, his forced enlisting, and he felt the same sour feeling in his gut that he'd felt back then.

"Will this take long? I'm rather busy."

"Not at all, Mr. Cooper. I'll only take a few minutes of your time. May I come in?"

Peter opened the door fully for the general and stepped aside. "Please don't call me Mr. Cooper. Peter's fine."

"Very well, Peter. What a lovely house you have here."

"Thanks," replied Peter insincerely, as he led the general into the living room.

They chose opposite chairs and sat in silence for a long moment before Peter said, "Uh, can I get you a glass of something?"

"No thank you, Peter. Hopefully, this will not take long."

"Well then, what can I do for you?" asked Peter.

"Do you remember me at all, Peter? We met many years ago."

As soon as the general mentioned it, Peter noticed a slight tic in the general's demeanor that triggered a small bit of recognition... But he lied, "Sorry. You don't look familiar."

"Well, that doesn't surprise me," said the general with a smile. "It was back when you enlisted. I was a staff sergeant stationed at the admin office. I administered your ASVAB."

"Okay. I *might* remember seeing you there," Peter admitted.

"Well, as you can see from the shiny star here," the general pointed to the brigadier general star on his uniform, "I've had a few promotions since then. I'm now Brigadier General Harrison Applegate."

Applegate. That was the name that was on the tip of his lying brain.

"And in a strange sort of way, I'm actually here to talk to you about that day twenty-two years ago."

"How so?" asked Peter, his interest reluctantly piqued.

"The ASVAB exam tests ten separate categories, as you may recall. The scores you had in each of those categories are combined to get an overall score. Your score was a 94, where the minimum to enter the army at the time was 31. In short, Peter, you were far above the norm. And by all accounts you were very successful at your job. Yet you only stayed in the army for four years. Why is that?"

'I'm not real sure, to tell you the truth. I enjoyed my tour in Germany, and I made a few friends while enlisted. I guess... military life was just not my style."

"And life after the military, how has that been for you?"

Peter sat and contemplated that for a moment. Life had been great after the military. He'd met the love of his life. He'd had two great children, and a rewarding career. But then came the three-year decline into hell, and he was not about to discuss that.

"Life has had its ups and downs." Peter didn't offer any more than that.

"To be honest, Peter, I already know a considerable amount about you and your life since the military. I've been keeping tabs on you."

The army had been keeping tabs on him? "Why?"

"Because, Peter. You are a bright,

intelligent man; far more intelligent than you give yourself credit for. Your entrance exams were exceptional, to say the least, but you scored particularly high in one area. Off the charts, as a matter of fact."

There were several moments of silence as this information penetrated Peter's mind. The general sat across from Peter, arms to his side, and not once did he take his eyes off him.

"Why are you telling me this now?" Peter demanded. "Why didn't you tell me this back then, if it's so important to you? I'm no longer in the army and I'm not going back. What does it matter anymore?"

"Would it have made a difference if I'd told you this twenty-two years ago when you enlisted? Would you have stayed in the army longer with this information? Would you have still married? Would you still have become an architect? Would Mary still have died in an auto accident?"

All these questions floated through the air, but Peter flinched at the mention of Mary. Mary was his wife's given name, and anyone that knew her called her Minnie. Hearing her name spoken out loud felt like an ice pick in the heart.

Peter was confused and irritated. "What's

the point of all this?" he asked, angrily.

"Peter, I clearly have more knowledge about you than just the basics. I know you are about to lose this house. I know your kids are barely passing their classes. I know you were laid off, and are currently looking for work. What if I told you that I could drastically change your circumstances, almost instantly?"

Peter was a proud man. To hear a stranger plainly spell out everything that he was struggling with almost brought him to tears. He had failed, and he was embarrassed. He was far too ashamed to ask for help from anyone.

"Are you sure I can't get you something to drink? I'm going to get myself a scotch." Peter stood without waiting for the general to reply and walked to the bar cabinet. He pulled out the bottle of Glenfiddich and two glasses. He returned to his seat and poured out two fingers each.

"Peter, this is not the answer to your problems," said the general as he took the glass from Peter.

"It might not be the answer, but it might help ease the process."

Peter brought the glass to his lips and tilted it back until the glass was again empty.

The general sipped at his glass and returned it to the table. Peter poured himself another and leaned back, glass in hand.

"So, what do I have to do to get this 'help' that you're offering?"

"Before I can really tell you more about that, I have to have your word that you will not divulge any of the information that we are to discuss to anyone. Not even your children—although I don't think they would believe any of it. I have to be clear here: no one. No one at all."

Peter held up his hand, his pinky finger pressed against his thumb and said with mock solemnity, "Scout's honor."

"I'm sorry Peter, but I'll need more than that. I have a confidentiality agreement that you would need to sign. What I am about to tell you is beyond top-secret-level clearance." The general opened his attaché case and removed a file folder with the words "EYES ONLY" on the cover. From it, he slid out two sheets of finely typed paper. He handed one of them to Peter, then sat back in his chair and again sipped his scotch. As Peter read over the forms, the general finally took his eyes off of Peter and scanned the living room. He was quite surprised to find the house in good order, considering all of Peter's troubles, including raising two teenage children alone.

After several minutes of silent reading, Peter looked up at the general and said, "This must be seriously top secret if the army would go to these extremes, were I to talk. Do you have a pen?"

The general produced a blue-marbled Mont Blanc pen and Peter signed the document before returning it to the general.

"Actually, Peter, this isn't an army operation. It's an unclassified branch of the government that only a very select few even know exists. It's so clandestine that I'm currently not at liberty to inform you of its call sign. The document that you just signed will only afford you just enough information to make a rational decision whether or not to assist us; no more than that. If you agree, there will be several more documents that will need to be signed along the way. Do you understand?"

Peter nodded.

"Good. Now that we have an understanding, and your signature, we are inviting you to join a small team of exclusively selected civilians, others such as yourself, to travel back in time. Back to 1942, France to be precise."

CHAPTER 5

Visibly stunned, Peter sat in silence. Not sure if what General Applegate was saying was a joke, he said, "Come again?"

Applegate smiled. "You heard me correctly, Peter. We want to send you back in time. Back to 1942. Without disclosing too many overly complicated details, we have found—hypothetically, that is—a way to time travel, and there is something that we would like the team to accomplish back in 1942. Something so simplistic, yet so monumental, that life as we know it could possibly be changed forever."

Peter slumped back into his chair, his mind reeling from the words escaping the general's mouth. He looked down at the empty scotch glass and wondered if the alcohol had anything to do with how outrageous this whole scenario was. He mentally shrugged off the thought and focused on General Applegate. Was he telling him the truth, or was this all some kind of ruse? Then the words started to hit him, as if on a time delay. "Wait—hypothetically?" scoffed Peter.

"Well, yes. The technology allowing us to travel in time is limited. Meaning, we are confident that we can send our team to 1942 and retrieve them back to the present; but only once. Obviously, once put into motion, we are committing to a certain number of events that will begin to unfold. You, Peter, are the last team member necessary to complete this operation. If you agree to participate, you will be one of four in total that will be going on the mission. You, an associate with similar ties to the military, and two scientists. The two scientists were chosen to ensure you have passage back to the present. You and your associate will focus on the mission. It's simple, really."

"Simple? You call going back in time and changing some event simple? How safe is this 'hypothetical' device? If you can't test it, how are you sure that it will work? And more importantly, how are we guaranteed that it'll be able to bring us back?"

General Applegate merely nodded at each of the questions. When he was sure Peter was finished, he replied. "Again, without divulging classified information, we are very confident that the mission will be successful. Once you commit, everything that is pertinent will be disclosed to you."

Peter shook his head. "I just don't know. Why are you asking *me*? I am sure there are a hundred other candidates currently in the military that can handle this mission much better then I can. As you said, I've got many personal issues to deal with already, and I'm not sure that adding one more to the list will make my life any better."

"First off, the reason we selected you for this mission relates to your ASVAB scores. Your scores from twenty-two years ago have been flagged for many potential missions over the years. With many of those missions, I have proposed adding you to the team, and each time, my superiors have rejected it. This is your chance, Peter."

"Rejected? Why?"

General Applegate's eyes darted to the side and then back to Peter. "Because of your legal issues prior to enlisting. Nothing more."

"What?! Those were supposed to have been removed from my record if I enlisted. You mean they're still there?"

"I'm afraid so, Peter. They're not on your

civilian records, but they will always be in your government file. No getting around that."

Again, Peter sat in silence, attempting to comprehend everything the general was telling him. Peter had long ago believed that his juvenile escapades of stealing cars and dabbling with drugs were no more than a bad memory. He was assured at the time by his father's attorney that the whole mess would be "cleansed" from his record if he joined the army. To hear that it still existed worried him. It was all quite overwhelming.

"Peter, you don't need to decide today. Take some time to think it over. This is a big decision. Just remember, you cannot discuss this with anyone, but you do need to think it through completely."

"How long is this mission expected to take? As you so astutely pointed out, I have personal issues that need immediate attention. More importantly, why should I trust you?"

"The mission should be completed in less than three months, from start to finish. You will need training and be completely *read-in* on the entire mission, and that is expected to take six weeks. The overall time you will be away will be four months. In that time, I am prepared to take care of all of your financial obligations, including stopping all foreclosure actions against you. I will also arrange for proper care for your children while you are away. As to why you should trust me, I'm offering a solution to a majority of your problems, beginning with the financial. I believe you have found no other avenues to provide solutions to these issues. Not to mention, this will be the greatest adventure on which any human being has ever embarked."

"God, my children. What'll they think is happening? Where will they go?"

"We are aware of your situation. We know, as I've said, that your wife died in an automobile accident twenty-one months ago. In that time, you have not contacted Mary's parents once. I would imagine that they would love to see their grandchildren. And perhaps that would help the children to let go of some of their anger toward you. I understand that they are both quite rebellious right now?"

"That's an understatement," replied Peter. "How is it you know so much about me?"

"As I said earlier, I've been keeping tabs on you. Since the first time I met you, I believed there was a spark of brilliance inside you. Your test scores supported my hypothesis. Unfortunately, my direct superior back then is still my direct superior now. He still feels I am wasting my time with you, but I have lobbied hard for you, and he finally conceded.

"In fact, you and I both have a lot riding on this operation. I am taking leave from the army because of this mission. This is an unsanctioned mission, and there cannot be any paper trail whatsoever that could lead back to the government."

"If not backed by the government, who'll be taking care of my financial commitments?"

"That would be me."

"You? Why would you do that?"

"Because, Peter. I feel that strongly about this mission. The lives that it could positively affect are worldwide. The entire global economy could be profoundly affected in a positive way. By how much, nobody knows."

"Two weeks? You need to know within two weeks?" asked Peter.

"We would like to know much sooner than that. The training begins in about a month. Should you choose to decline, I will still need to fill your spot on the mission."

"Understandable," agreed Peter. "What about pay? Will you also be paying for my time on the mission?"

"There will be no pay, Peter. I will be personally paying all your bills, along with getting the mortgage payments caught up. That alone should be plenty of compensation for your time and effort. Besides, you will be doing this for your country. That should be reward enough."

"To hell with your 'for my country' crap. If my country gave a shit about me, they would have told me about my skill set when I enlisted and given me a better job than a cook's assistant, and not held it in some general's pocket until they needed my help," shot back Peter, surprising both himself and General Applegate.

"I can understand your anger, Peter. I'm sorry that it had to be done this way. But if not for your country, consider this: the changes you make on this mission may very well affect your life in ways that neither of us can comprehend. We don't know for sure what will happen after the changes on the mission transpire. It could be nothing, or it could be amazing. I would ask that you consider it."

Peter took in these last words, and agreed that if what the general was saying came to fruition, his life could be better all around. If this mission could improve the global economy, maybe he wouldn't be in the financial crisis that had developed over the last few years. "All right, General. I'll think about it. I'll let you know by the end of the week, one way or the other."

They both stood up, and Peter led the general to the door. But before Peter had the door open, the general opened his attaché case once more, this time producing an envelope and handing it to Peter.

"Here's a little something for your time and consideration. I understand your unemployment has run out. This should help you out until you come to a decision." He left before Peter had a chance to open the envelope.

CHAPTER 6

Peter stepped back into the house, pondering the absurdity of the last thirty minutes of his life. Time travel, he wondered. Was it even possible? If it was, could he actually change the future? These questions would have to remain unanswered, for the moment at least. He dropped the unopened envelope onto the coffee table next to the bottle of scotch. Seeing the bottle, he decided another drink would help calm his mind.

With a refreshed drink in hand, he paced around the house. Peter often paced when his mind was working. Minnie use to tease him about "wearing a path in the carpet." What would she do? She was the adventurous type, and Peter thought she would most definitely go for it. But he was not his wife. Regardless of his failures since her death, he had to remain somewhat responsible for his kids.

The kids. What would they think? He

knew he couldn't tell them about it, so how would he answer their questions? Questions about why he would be leaving for four months, maybe longer. On the bright side, Minnie's parents could be a part of their lives again. He had tried many times to get his in-laws involved with the kids' lives, but every time he picked up the phone to call them, he'd stopped halfway through dialing their number. He just couldn't swallow his pride long enough to ask for their help, let alone help from anyone else.

As he paced around the house, sipping his scotch, he heard the familiar click of the front door. He walked into the foyer and was surprised to see Brett.

"Brett? Everything okay? Why are you home early?" Peter glanced down at his wristwatch; it was just after one o'clock.

"The nurse sent me home. The school tried to call, but they said the phone had been disconnected. I'm having another migraine." Brett dropped his backpack next to the sofa and tossed the day's mail on the coffee table. "Can we call the doctor now? This is the third time this month that I've been sent home with a migraine. I think something's wrong."

"Sure thing, kiddo. I'll call and see if I can

get an appointment for later this week. Why don't you head up and get in bed. I'll bring up some aspirin."

Brett just nodded and sluggishly climbed the stairs to his room.

Peter stood in the hall, staring up the stairs, wondering where he could get the money for another doctor visit. He finished his scotch in one swallow and headed to the bathroom to get Brett some aspirin.

Once Brett was seen to, Peter returned to the living room to tidy up a bit. He returned the bottle of scotch to the liquor cabinet and picked up the mail that Brett had brought in when he got home. It was the usual: bills and ads. He tossed them back onto the coffee table and opened the envelope from Applegate. Inside was a stack of hundred-dollar bills. Peter sank into a chair as he began to count them. He counted out twenty crisp hundred-dollar bills. Peter smiled and thought his week was taking a turn for the better.

CHAPTER 7

With Tori at a sleepover, and Brett quietly moping in his room, Peter decided to go out to the bar. After changing clothes, he stopped in his study and pulled a few hundred-dollar bills from the general's envelope. It had been a while since he had gone out, and he felt that his recent windfall was as good a reason as any to celebrate.

He was pretty upbeat considering everything that had been happening lately, especially that day. He decided that this monetary bonus would not go to waste. So, with pep in his step he moved vigorously through the house and out the front door. The nine-block walk did his mind good. As he headed down the sidewalk, he thought about what life would be like in 1942. Could he fit in enough to not draw suspicion? What if someone caught him and found out he was from the future? He giggled. He realized that if the police picked up some guy today that claimed he was from the future, they'd think he was from the loony bin.

As he crossed the street, he glanced down and noticed a penny lying next to the curb. He leaned over and picked it up. He inspected it with the idea of adding it to Brett's coin collection, if it was worth anything. He flipped it over and noticed that it was a wheat penny. Flipping it back over, he looked at the front more closely: 1947. He chuckled, and thought how ironic it would have been if the penny were from the same year as the mission. That's when Peter paused. He smiled as he slid the penny into his pocket. A plan was starting to form in his mind. A plan, *his* plan, which could change *his* future.

Even though it had been four months since he had last been there, Peter sauntered into Herb's Corner Pub like it was yesterday. Joe, the evening bartender, looked up and smiled at Peter as he approached the bar.

"Howdy, stranger! It's been some time since we've seen hide or hair of you. Pull up a chair."

Peter smiled as he slid onto the only available bar stool. "Hey, Joe."

"What brings you in this fine evening?" asked Joe as he started to pour Peter a drink.

"Still scotch and water?"

Peter nodded. "Oh, nothing too much. Just thought it would be good to get out. It *has* been a while."

"Well, you've been missed, that's for certain. Benny's been asking about you. So has Stella." Joe slid Peter's drink across the bar, eyeing his expression. "How are the kids?"

"You know. Teenage know-it-alls. Nothing I can't handle." Peter paused to sip his drink, then continued. "Can you believe Tori wants to get her nose pierced? Seriously? Everyone wants to get perforated these days."

"My kid got her nose done first, then it was her tongue, and just a month ago she got her eyebrow done. I thought about putting my foot down, but I could tell in her eyes that if I said no, she'd go ahead and just do it anyway. Granted, she's seventeen, but I still hate seein' it."

"Tell me about it, Joe. Tell me about it."

"Are you working yet? I imagine unemployment won't last much longer."

Peter winced at the topic. Being unemployed for the last eighteen months had been rough, and his mood on the topic had not been great. But Peter pushed away the negative thoughts in his mind and said, "I haven't found anything yet, but I have a promising lead. That's why I came here tonight, to sort of celebrate." Once the words were out of his mouth, he realized that he had already decided to take the mission. He smiled to himself and took a long sip of his scotch.

"Well, that's great news, Peter. First one's on the house, then!" Joe smiled at him and moved to the other end of the bar to fill a drink order.

Peter sat in silence, briefly scanning the room to see if he recognized anyone. To his surprise, the atmosphere hadn't changed at all. The same tacky vinyl booths lined the outside wall, and that tear in the pool table felt still hadn't been fixed. He felt comfortable in his local dive bar. He turned back to his drink and noticed a reflection, in the mirror behind the bar of a woman staring back at him. Peter smiled, lifted his drink toward her reflection, and then took a sip. She returned his smile then looked away, her eyes darting to something across the bar. Peter continued to look in her direction as he tried to place her familiar face, but she didn't return his gaze. He supposed it was her pleasant, but remarkable profile. She reminded him of... His recollection was interrupted as a man walked up and sat across from her. They whispered briefly, before he nonchalantly glanced up to the bar. Without focusing on anyone in particular, his eyes landed on Peter momentarily as he scanned the place. Peter noticed the not-so-obvious glance from the stranger. The two sitting in the booth were obviously discussing him. He began to wonder if the general had had him followed. But before he could give it another thought, he was tapped on the shoulder.

Peter turned his bar stool to see Stella Fryer standing behind him. Stella stood a gracious five feet, two inches tall, and wore a jean miniskirt. She wore three-inch black pumps, which greatly improved her height. Her top was slightly sheer, and he could see the outline of her black bra beneath. Her ruby red painted lips smiled ear to ear, and parted to say, "Long time, no see, handsome."

"Hello, Stella. It has been a while." Stella was a few years older than Peter, and was the only woman that he had considered romantically since Minnie died. But something always delayed Peter from acting on his visual attraction. He wasn't sure if it was her over-flirtatious personality that stopped him, or if it was the fact that she was the local "bar ornament" with a moderately slutty disposition. After many nights spent drowning his sorrows there, he never saw her leave with another man. Still, Peter found it difficult to make a move. "I'd offer you a seat, but as you can see, all full."

"Don't worry about it, baby. Grab your drink and come back to my booth. I've got someone I want you to meet anyway."

Stella was the one person Peter didn't want to see tonight. The last time he was there, he and Stella had a few too many drinks, and things moved a bit too far, too fast. She knew he was still suffering the loss of his wife, and he told her he wasn't ready, but Stella pushed and pushed and had her hands down his pants most of that late night. Stella was a good part of the reason why he'd stopped going into Herb's—that, plus his lack of discretionary income. That had been four months ago.

"I would love to come back to your booth, Stella, but..." Peter paused to think of the right words to communicate the messages "not interested" and "no chance in hell" without hurting her feelings. "It's just that I need to talk with Benny, and Joe thinks he'll be here any moment," lied Peter. "Maybe later?"

Stella turned on a heel and ambled back

to her table. Peter felt bad for being so blunt with her, but he was still not in a place where he felt comfortable, romantically, with another woman. Deep inside, he still felt devoted to Minnie, even though enough time had passed. Benny would tell him "Just sleep with her, already" anytime Stella would hang around them. Benny's thought on the matter was "It's just sex." Maybe Benny was right, thought Peter. Maybe he should just sleep with another woman—maybe he would feel better for it. Maybe with another woman not named Stella.

Peter chuckled to himself about the thought as he downed the last of his scotch. He flagged Joe down for another. Joe nodded and held up his finger indicating it would be a minute. While he waited, Peter began to review the conversation with the general again in his mind. Could it all be possible? Could time travel actually work? Peter recalled reading many science fiction stories where time travel was possible, but only if you didn't change the past. But that was exactly what the general was proposing. What if he went back to make this small change, and it ended up making a much bigger transformation than anyone ever considered? He surmised that the think tank behind the mission had to have already given that a lot of thought if they were moving forward with the program.

Completely lost in his thoughts, Peter didn't see Joe slide his drink in front of him. Peter picked up the drink and toasted him. Joe returned the nod and continued about his business. Peter raised the glass to his nose to smell the woody notes he was so fond of. He took a long drink, savoring the burn as it went down. Peter was not a lush, but the day demanded drinking. This was now his fifth or sixth drink for the day, and he was feeling a bit fuzzy. Granted, they were spread out through the day, but it was a nice buzz nonetheless. It was a good feeling after so many months of self-control.

The longer Peter sat alone, the more the loneliness started to creep in. He was really hoping that Benny would have been there by now. What were his options to kill the boredom? He could strike up a conversation with one of the strangers to his left or to his right—both of whom were deep in conversation with others. He could venture back and talk with Stella. He knew where that would lead: having Stella play footsie with him beneath the table, and possibly getting blown in the parking lot. Or he could sit and wait until Benny or somebody else he knew arrived. He tossed back the remaining few swallows of his drink and flagged Joe for another. He would wait. It had been a long time since he and Benny had talked, and he had things on his mind that he could only share with Benny.

As Peter waited, he peered into the reflection in the mirror to see if the couple was still in the booth across the bar. The booth was now empty, and once he noticed it, he turned and looked around the bar to see if they had moved or just left. He found them sitting in the corner booth with Stella. From what Peter could see, they were in a deep conversation and Stella did not look comfortable.

Peter looked over at Joe and waved him over. "Hey Joe, you see those two talking with Stella?" Peter tilted his head in their direction. "Have you seen them here before?"

Joe, not the most discreet person, flipped his head in their direction. "Nope. First time I've seen them was tonight. They came in right about the same time as you. Why do you ask?"

"I noticed them earlier and they seemed to be watching my every move. Kind of creeps me out." As he told this to Joe, he began to develop a plan—an alcohol-induced plan at that. He leaned closer to Joe and whispered into his ear. As Peter continued to talk, Joe's solemn expression turned into a devious smile. He nodded and said he'd play along.

CHAPTER 8

"What do you mean I can't have another drink?" Peter exclaimed loudly, while standing up so quickly his bar stool tipped back and crashed to the floor, grabbing the attention of everyone in the bar.

"I'm cutting you off, Pete. You've had enough. I can get you a cup of coffee or you can find another place to get a drink." Joe winked ever so slightly.

"No, no. It's fine. I was losing my fondness for thish plashe anyway. I think I'll take my hard-earned money to Charlie's over on Seventeenth. He never turns away my money." Peter grabbed his glass and took the last swallow and tossed the glass to the floor, breaking it into dozens of pieces. "Now, I'll leave."

Peter peripherally glanced around the bar, ensuring he had the appropriate eyes on him before he turned for the door and stumbled out. Once the door closed, he ran straight for the alley and ducked out of sight. Standing in the shadows of the dark alley, he leaned around the corner to get a good view of the front of the bar. Moments later, the couple burst out of the double doors in pursuit of Peter. He held back until they crossed the street and got into a nondescript black sedan before he turned and walked down the alley. Peter entered the back door of Herb's, completely unnoticed.

Through the back door, he found himself face to face with Stella.

"Oh Peter, what have you gotten yourself into?" cried Stella, with an overly concerned look on her face.

"Gotten myself into? What are you talking about?"

"Those two! They cornered me in my booth and they really gave me the willies. They kept asking me questions about you and how well I knew you. What's going on, Peter?"

"I've never seen those guys before in my life. I caught them watching me earlier, and then when Joe and I noticed that they were talking with you, we devised a plan to get them out of the pub. I'm not sure who they were, or what they wanted, but I'm glad they're gone."

"Oh, Peter!" exclaimed Stella as she thrust herself into his open arms, hugging him. "I was so scared."

Not knowing exactly how to react to Stella

hugging him, he lightly patted her on the back and said, "There, there. It'll be all right."

She continued the hug for a few moments, but when it became a little too awkward, Peter began to pull away. "Not yet, baby." Stella said. "I like feeling your warmth."

"I should at least go check with Joe. Make sure he's not pissed at me for breaking his glass."

"Okay, baby. Come back to my booth soon," replied Stella, and then walked into the ladies' room. Peter realized he also had to pee, so before heading back up front, he stopped in the men's room to take care of business.

When Peter emerged from the back hallway, he was met with a round of applause from the entire bar, and Joe was grinning ear to ear. He must not have been too bent about the broken glass. Peter gave an embarrassed wave to everyone, and the applause began to die down. With everyone returning to their own devices, he made his way back to his bar stool and sat back down. Joe made his way over to him, then pointed to the booth where the two strangers were seated earlier. Peter's eyes followed Joe's pointed finger and found Benny sitting alone, staring back at him.

"Benny!" Peter called out across the crowded bar.

"The one and only. I hear I missed quite the

performance from you."

"Joe, another scotch for myself and whatever Benny is drinking. Oh, and a couple shots of whatever you got handy. Can you send the drinks over to the booth?"

"Sure thing, Pete." Joe started mixing fresh drinks.

Peter walked over and slid into the empty seat across from Benny. "How the hell are you, buddy? It's been way too long."

"I can't complain. The powers-that-be at work have been keeping me busy. Just when I think I'm getting ahead of things, I get a new load of crap dumped on my plate."

Benny hadn't changed. It had only been four months, but Peter thought everyone was going to be different when he came in tonight. Everyone was exactly the same. Maybe it was just him that was changing.

"Well, at least you've got a job, you schmuck," Peter teased.

"Yeah, sorry 'bout that. Any luck on the job front?" Benny's look became a bit too somber for Peter's liking.

"I've got some things in the works. Great things, Benny. That's kind of why I came in tonight. I wanted to talk to you about some things. Where the hell have you been?"

"Long story, buddy. Short version, I was having a few drinks at, uh... hold on." Benny paused as Joe brought drinks.

"Hey Joe, could you bring us a few more shots? Tequila this time, and no training wheels either," asked Peter.

Joe nodded and returned to the bar.

"Shots? Peter, I'm already a bit too liquored up to have shots."

"Trust me, with what I've got to say, you'll need these, plus a few more. So, you were telling me where you were before?"

"No, no. No changing the subject like that. What's this big news you've got to share?"

Peter leaned back, looking at Benny, wondering how much he should share about the mission. He had to talk to somebody about it, and Benny was his go-to guy. He'd been there for Peter through all his troubles the last few years. Benny was his best friend and had a good head on his shoulders. He couldn't tell his kids. Stella wasn't bright enough to understand what the offer meant. Yes, it had to be Benny.

"Tell me, Benny. What do you know about 1942?" asked Peter, before he tossed back a shot.

CHAPTER 9

It was the third succession of heavy knocks that finally woke Peter from the dead. He had been dreaming about rare coins, Stella's ruby red lips and shots of tequila.

A loud knock-knock-knock was heard throughout the house.

"Brett!" Peter yelled. "Can you go see who that is?"

Not hearing an acknowledgment, he wondered if his son had heard him. He pushed the sheets off himself and swung his legs to the floor as he sat up. He stretched, then leaned over, resting his face in the palms of his hands, reliving the night before. He felt like crap, and once again, he mentally swore off drinking heavily ever again. It was an all-too-familiar agreement that he'd made with himself over the last few years. And each time, the self-imposed deal was broken for one reason or another.

Peter sat on the side of his bed for several more minutes before Brett came into his room.

"Dad? There's some guy here to see you. He says you know him? General Applesomething."

"Thanks, kiddo. Tell him I'll be down in a few minutes."

"Do you really know him? He's got a couple people with him, and Dad, they look kind of familiar."

"Familiar how?"

"I don't know. Almost like I've seen 'em before, but I can't remember where."

"Okay, well, I'll tell you and your sister all about it later. Can you make some coffee and offer them some? I'll be down in a minute."

Brett nodded and closed the door as he left. Peter glanced at the clock: 11:35. He was surprised by how late it was, but not as surprised as he was about the general's visit. He thought he had a full week to decide whether to accept the mission or not.

Not wanting to fall back asleep, he forced himself to get up. He grabbed the pile of clothes from the night before and went into the bathroom to clean himself up.

As he washed and brushed his teeth quickly, his mind replayed the events from the night before. Most of the night was pretty clear. He remembered talking with Joe. He remembered avoiding Stella's advances far too many times. He remembered making some kind of scene and breaking a glass. *Why did I do that?*, he wondered. He remembered talking to Benny, but couldn't remember everything they talked about. He sort of recalled talking about old pennies for some reason, but he couldn't be sure.

Peter rinsed the toothpaste from his mouth and spat. He looked at himself in the mirror and felt like he was missing something important from last night. He again tried to retrace his steps from the night before. There was something about Stella... but he couldn't pull the memory into view. He remembered her hugging him and thanking him for something. What was it?

He turned from the mirror and grabbed his clothes. He pulled on his jeans and slid his arms into the button-up shirt, all the while thinking about Stella and the hug. He turned back to the mirror to run his fingers through his hair, and that's when it hit him. Everything began to rush into his mind at the same time. The couple that was at the bar.

The image of their faces in his mind was so much clearer now, and he strangely felt a familiarity with them—like he had seen them before. But where?

Back in his bedroom, he slid his feet into his loafers and walked toward his bedroom door. As he reached for the handle, he paused a moment, still thinking about the couple. Could they have been the two walking into the ice cream shop the day before? As he recalled the memory of them walking in, he was positive that they were the same couple from the bar. He wasn't completely positive, but he also felt like he may have seen them other places throughout the week. He was being followed. He was sure of it now. He pulled open the door and walked down the stairs, determined to get some answers from Applegate.

CHAPTER 10

Peter was dumbfounded at what he saw when he walked into the living room. He was expecting to see the general and two other people, as Brett had mentioned. Just not the general and... the same couple that had been following him around over the last week.

"Peter. Sorry to drop in unannounced, but we need to talk," the general said as he stood up to greet Peter.

"That's fine, General, but I thought I had a bit of time to think the offer through," Peter replied, not looking at him, but at the two others in the room.

"That's why I'm here, Peter. I'm afraid the decision now needs to be made immediately— because of your indiscretions last night."

"What do you mean? I don't think my discretions from last night are of any of your business."

"Oh, but they are, Peter. You made them

my concern when you talked about the mission to your friends. Benny and Stella, was it?"

Peter flinched noticeably upon hearing his friends' names. Clearly, the two others in the room did in fact work for the general, and had been there to keep tabs on his movements. This sudden realization pissed him off.

'First off, I've not told anyone about the mission. Second, what gives you the right to have me followed around?" he snapped, while gesturing towards the general's companions.

"Calm down, Peter. There's no need to get upset." Applegate smiled while waving him toward a seat.

"Peter, I would like you to meet a couple of people. They are not the bad guys. This is Julie. She has recently signed onto the mission." Applegate turned from the woman to the man next to her. "And this here is Mark. He's part of the security detail that everyone on the mission is assigned. If you accept, security personnel will be assigned to you as well."

Peter finally took his eyes off of the couple and looked directly at General Applegate. "Is all this security really necessary? If nobody knows about the mission, why would they matter?"

"To be blunt, Peter, it is because of actions like the ones you undertook last night. We have to be absolutely sure not one word gets out regarding the mission."

"I understand that, but a heads-up would have been nice. And for what it's worth, I didn't say a word to anyone about anything," Peter exclaimed, hoping his actions from last night would not betray his spotty memory.

"That was a pretty crafty scheme that you and the bartender pulled last night," Julie said, speaking for the first time, a slight smile attempting to cross her face. "It wasn't until we tracked down Charlie's clear across town that we realized you'd given us the slip.

"Yeah, about that. I wasn't sure what to think about you two. I would have bought you a drink if I had known you were only there to babysit me." As Peter said this, Julie broke his eye contact and looked away, obviously embarrassed. Mark, on the other hand, stared directly into Peter's eyes, his gaze unwavering.

Peter watched the body language of his visitors, and realized that all three were relaxed. It was only him that was uptight. Just the night before, he was nearly positive he was going to take the mission. Now, he wasn't so sure. The whole mess was a bit too cloak-and-dagger for his liking. There was silence in the room as these thoughts crossed Peter's mind.

"Peter, how can we really know for sure you haven't mentioned anything to your friends?"

"Is my word not good enough for you?"

"Honestly, Peter, no it's not. Mark feels that you may have compromised the mission by talking with your friend Benedict Welsh, and—"

Peter stopped the general. "You can forget that right now. Benny knows nothing. I'll give you that it may have looked suspicious last night. To tell the truth, I'd just about decided to accept your offer before I went to the bar. It had been several months since I'd been out, and I knew that if I did in fact go on your mission, it would be a while before I would be seeing my friends again. I just wanted to see them one last time before..."

Peter trailed off. As he spoke, he realized that he could potentially lose everything he had—his family, his friends—if the mission failed. And for all he knew, he could possibly lose everything if the mission was actually a success as well. Up to that point he had thought only of how the mission could help him. Digging out of the financial hole he'd been in for the last two years had been his main motivation. He'd never really thought about how this decision would affect so many other people. What he'd earlier thought of as being a simple decision, he now saw was a life-altering resolution.

Peter stood and began to pace about the room. The eyes of the general and his companions followed his every step. He was, again, re-evaluating everything the general had to offer. He just wished he knew more about what kind of effect time travel would have on him and his life. He thought about pouring himself a drink, but ruled out the idea just as quickly.

"Peter? Everything okay?" asked Applegate.

At the sound of the general's voice, Peter felt like he was being overly scrutinized, everyone watching him. "Can we speak privately, General? Do they need to be here?" Peter said, pointing to Julie and Mark.

"Not a problem, Peter," he replied. He turned to the couple. "Why don't you two go grab a coffee around the corner. I'll call you when we're finished."

Julie and Mark stood and silently walked toward the door. As they did so, Julie paused near Peter and gave him a reassuring smile. Moments later, the door clicked shut, and Peter and the general were alone.

"Now, is this better, Peter?"

"Much." He sat down across from the general and tried to recall everything that he had planned on asking. "I have some more questions, if you don't mind."

"By all means, Peter. If I can answer them, I certainly will."

"First off, if I go back in time, and happen to die, what will happen to my kids in the present?"

"As I understand it, Peter, your children will only know that you died in your training cover story. They will know nothing about your time travel mission."

"Okay, about that. If I accept, I want a college trust in place for both of them. I also want my house paid off. If I'm going back in time, risking my life on a hypothetical mission, I want some assurances that my family will be taken care of."

"Don't get me wrong, Peter. I completely understand where you're coming from on this matter. I will certainly agree to those requirements for you, but I have to tell you: they will not matter."

Peter was stunned. "Not matter? How can

it not matter? They're my children, for Christ's sake. They absolutely matter!"

"I'm sorry, Peter. You misunderstood me. It won't matter if I pay off the house, or pay for their college today, because once you go back in time, you will instantly alter how history will advance from the moment you make a single change in 1942. You see, once you change something in the past, the future might not be the same as you remember. Your memories—as well as the memories of everyone else going on the mission—will remain in place, as they will be *linear* to you and only you. But for any of us staying in this present, well, we will have no recollection of the events happening up to that point. Our memories will shift at the point when you and your team come back."

The general paused a moment to let Peter absorb what he was telling him. "The dynamic of you and the team going on the mission will allow you to maintain your memories, as if they actually happened. But in reality… they never did. You could come back to a world where you are single, or married to another person entirely."

"Why didn't you tell me any of this before?" Peter demanded.

"Because if I did, you may not have

considered the mission in the first place. Listen, Peter. According to our calculations, the mission has nothing but upside potential for all of civilization. If you go back and complete your mission successfully, our analysts assure me that your life will be very similar to, if not better than, the way it currently is. The algorithms that have been run on the success of the mission—run hundreds of times, I assure you—mostly result in you marrying Mary, and having two children."

"How can you know exactly who I would marry again if the mission is successful? Who is to say I don't find French women irresistible after the mission?"

"Just because you're going to France on the mission does not necessarily dictate that you will have a fondness for their women. You see, you're going back to 1942 from the present day. You will return to the *shifted* now. Your mission will have no influence on whom you will marry in-between. You will have not have been born in 1942, so, you will have no contact with yourself."

Peter's head ached from trying to wrap his mind around the whole theory of time travel. He closed his eyes and rubbed his temples.

"Peter, the odds are with you on this. You have to trust me."

"What exactly are the odds? Or are you not allowed to tell me that either?"

"No, unfortunately, I am not at liberty to discuss the exact odds with you, but believe me when I tell you, they are outstanding."

Peter broke down and crossed the room to the liquor cabinet and poured himself a scotch, despite the hangover. He wasn't sure of the exact cause of his headache anymore. He twirled the glass around in his hand, thinking about everything the general had just told him. He had been prepared to accept the mission, with all the promised benefits, yet without any concessions on the general's part. That was, until now.

"I'm sorry, General. I need more information. You tell me that I will have full access *if* I accept and sign the mission accord. I am not going to sign anything unless you give me the exact odds of success."

Now, it was the general that was silent. He sat for a long moment before speaking.

"The probability that you will have the same life and family upon your return..." the general paused momentarily before continuing, "...is fifty-five percent."

"Fifty-five percent?! How the hell is that an outstanding figure?"

"That is a fifty-five percent chance that you return to the same life as you have now. There are many other variables that directly affect those odds, and most of them are only positive. Your life when you return may very well be significantly better. Those odds are incalculable. Peter, you asked for the odds that your life will remain relatively the same. That is what I gave you."

Peter listened, and although he was working through a puzzle far beyond his understanding, he did realize one thing. During the entire conversation with the general, Peter had been gradually recalling more of the discussion from the night before, the one with Benny. He remembered the 1943 copper pennies, and he knew that they were *his* way of making the situation right for *him*, and him only. He would accept the mission and make sure he had some alone time back in 1942.

After several minutes of exaggerated reflection, Peter finally spoke.

"Okay, General. I know you say it won't matter, but I would like the college trust and the house paid for. Once those are taken care of, I'm in."

Peter looked Brigadier General Harrison Applegate in the eyes and smiled.

"When do we leave?"

BONUS CHAPTER
From Linear Shift, Part 2

The penetrating briskness of the thin night air chilled Peter to the bone. His eyes had adjusted to the darkness of a moonless sky. The few scattered streetlights shone harsh in contrast to the gloom throughout the village, their hardened light causing mysterious, foreboding shadows. The cobblestone streets were vacant, just as they had been all night, and the sound of silence was louder than the thoughts in his own mind.

Peter glanced at his night-glow watch, only to find ten minutes had passed since his last inspection. What, he wondered, are they waiting for? He shifted nervously in his crouch and decided it was time to move.

He crept stealthily along the stone wall that bordered the winding road. As he neared the edge of the shadows, he slowed his pace and briefly leaned into the glaring light to see if the street around the corner was vacant. To his surprise, he noticed the silhouette of another person slinking along the face of the building across the street. At first he could not clearly identify the individual. Then the shadowy figure also slipped into the light and Peter could make out the silhouette of a woman. He exhaled softly. He recognized the high cheekbones and silky brunette ponytail. It was his partner, Julie Frey.

Peter pursed his lips together and made a short bird chirp to attract her attention. Julie glanced around and, a moment later, returned the call. Peter once again checked his watch. Their time limit was critical; this mission needed to be complete inside of two hours. It was now 1:37 a.m., and it had been ninety-seven minutes since they entered the small French village. They had begun their incursion from separate ends, headed as discreetly as possible toward the same destination: the small café near the center of town. They were currently on opposite sides of the narrow street, just a few hundred feet away from their target, and Peter felt confident they would have no problem completing the mission with time to spare.

Cautiously, he stepped into the deserted

street and began to amble in Julie's direction, his leisurely pace belying his extreme nervousness about being exposed.

As Peter reached the halfway point, Julie also stepped onto the cobbled road and proceeded toward him. They met in a shadow at the edge of the light cast from the nearest light pole.

"Any problems on your end?" whispered Peter.

"I came across a few drunks stumbling out of a bar a few blocks over, but it was nothing I couldn't handle. You?"

"I haven't seen a soul all night. It's a little too perfect for comfort. Let's move before we're noticed."

With Julie at his side, Peter stepped from the shadows and walked confidently towards their destination. Despite the darkness, he could begin to make out the word *café* painted on the brick above the glass storefront. Seeing the familiar word, he instinctively relaxed; this was the closest they'd gotten all week.

With renewed energy Peter continued closer, but he stopped instantly when he heard the noise. Julie heard it too. It was the unmistakable sound of footfalls on the pavement. He could not tell which direction they were coming from, but he knew they were close. Their options were limited. They were out of cover and near the middle of the street. He intuitively reached out and took Julie's hand and began to walk in the opposite direction. As the two made it to the end of the block, they began to veer down a side street. But before they got around the corner, a loud voice startled them both.

"*Arrêter!*"

Peter's French was improving, and he recognized the word *stop*. He gripped Julie's hand tighter and halted. In unison, they turned to face the person behind the startling voice.

The man moving toward them was in the neighborhood of six and a half feet tall. His face was pockmarked and sported a wiry mustache. He was pointing a rifle in their general direction, and his uniform was clearly that of the Vichy France Army. "*Où vas-tu à cette heure de la nuit?*"

Peter understood the soldier's question– *Where are you going?*—but had been instructed to let Julie do all the talking.

"*Nous sommes tout simplement pour une balade. Belle nuit, n'est-ce pas?*" she replied perfectly. "We're just out for a stroll. Beautiful night, isn't it?"

"*à 1h40 du matin?*" The soldier directed the question at Peter. "At 1:40 in the morning?"

Peter simply nodded.

"*Que, chat a obtenu votre langue?*" The soldier asked if the cat had Peter's tongue.

Both Peter and Julie laughed out loud before Julie answered that Peter had a sore throat and the doctor had instructed him not to speak for several days. Peter nodded his head as Julie recited the scripted answer.

The soldier stood a few feet from them, still holding his rifle steady. He examined Peter before moving his eyes to Julie. As he raked his eyes over her feminine form, meticulously scrutinizing every luscious curve far longer than appropriate, Peter noticed how uncomfortable she was by the situation. Unfortunately, there wasn't anything he could do about it.

After visually molesting Julie, the soldier grinned slightly, and said, "*vous êtes plutôt sexuelle.*" Peter clinched his fists and stepped between Julie and the armed man.

The man raised his rifle to Peter's chest and demanded he get back: "*récupérer!*"

Julie placed her hand on Peter's shoulder and whispered, "It's not worth it."

Peter was about to step aside when the

soldier suddenly elbowed him in the face.

Peter dropped to his knees yelling, "Fuck! What did you do that for?" The words, in English, were out of his mouth before he could pull them back.

"*Américain soja*?" accused the soldier. Peter thought he was half right. He was American, but he was no spy. That part was obvious.

Peter stood back up and turned toward the soldier to explain, but the soldier jumped back and re-leveled his rifle at Peter's chest.

"Wait!" is all Peter could say before the soldier opened fire on him, shooting him three times in the torso. Julie screamed as Peter fell back, hitting the cobblestone street.

***

Lying on his back, Peter blinked his eyes. His head was throbbed where he cracked it against the pavement. He brought his hand to his chest and the pool of wetness he felt was not reassuring. When he lifted his hand, it was covered in red. He was shot. He tried to sit up, but Julie, kneeling next to him told him in English to wait a moment.

"Shh!" Peter whispered to her. "He'll hear you!"

"It's okay, Peter. The training is over. We failed again."

Training? Peter tried to sit up, but his head was spinning. Julie pushed on his shoulders in an effort to make him lie still, but he still managed to push up from the cobblestone street into a sitting position. He wobbled, then steadied himself and looked around. The scene—which had been dark just moments before—was in full daylight from the mercury-vapor lights above. He reached back and felt the growing knot on his head.

"What? But we were so close," Peter said.

"Yes, Peter. You were closer to your goal than you've been all week. But do you understand your error?" General Applegate asked as he stepped out of a doorway in the mock village.

Peter rolled to his side and got a leg underneath him. He stood up and looked menacingly over at Mark. The ogre was dressed in the Vichy uniform. "It's because that asshole crossed the line."

"There will be no lines in 1942. You have to expect anything and everything. Heaven forbid that you two encounter a soldier such as the one Mark was portraying." Applegate nodded to Mark, who returned the nod before turning to walk away. As he passed by Peter, he flashed a petulant smirk that grated on

Peter's nerves.

Peter forced himself to look at General Applegate. "Okay then. What would have been the correct reaction to Mark's sexual advances? Do we sacrifice Julie for the sake of the mission?"

"Don't be absurd, Peter. Julie has been through several levels of advanced combat training. The soldier would have suffered greater injury if he were to make that advance than he would from your efforts to play protector. Isn't that right, Julie?"

"Let's just say he would have to sit to pee for at least a week," replied Julie, now standing next to Peter. "But that was a very noble gesture," she said as she rubbed his shoulder.

"Right. Why don't you two get changed and wrap up for the day," suggested the general. "We'll discuss your results tomorrow."

Peter and Julie stood in silence as Applegate walked through the village and stepped into a dark alley.

"Are you going to be OK, Peter?" asked Julie, rubbing his shoulder again. "You hit your head pretty hard."

"Yeah, I'll be fine. My pride is what's really injured right now. I can't believe I let

Mark get to me like that. Seriously, did he have to hit me *and* shoot me?" asked Peter, not really looking for Julie to answer.

"Let's get this paintball goo cleaned off you and get out of here before Applegate changes his mind on more training."

ABOUT THE AUTHOR

When not writing, Paul is hard at work in the field of architecture. He has been in the field of design since 1992, and loves what he does. He lives with his wife and daughter in Littleton, Colorado, where he was born and raised.

To learn more about him and his books, visit www.Paul-Kohler.net